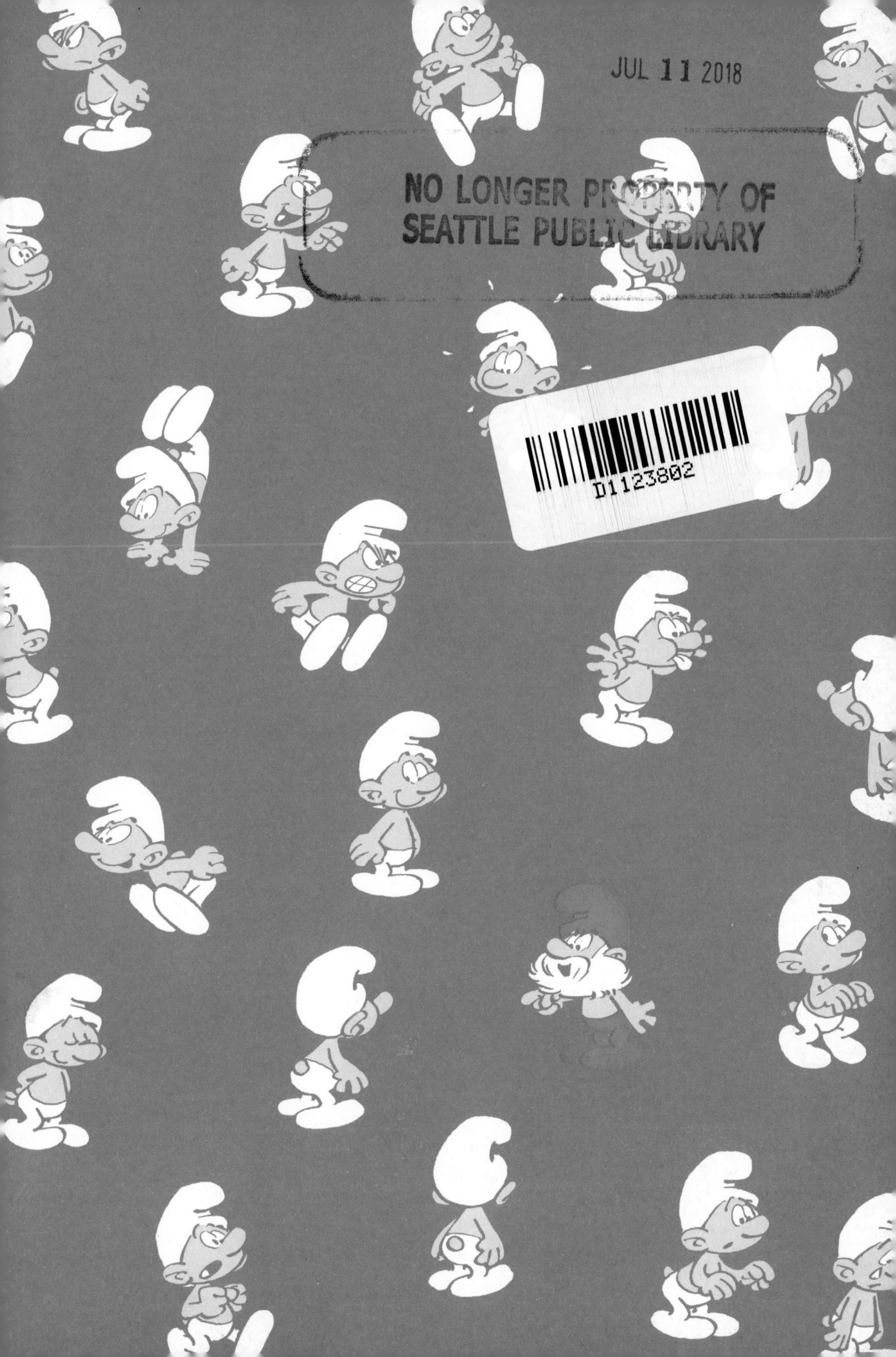

THE PURPLE SMURFS

Peyo

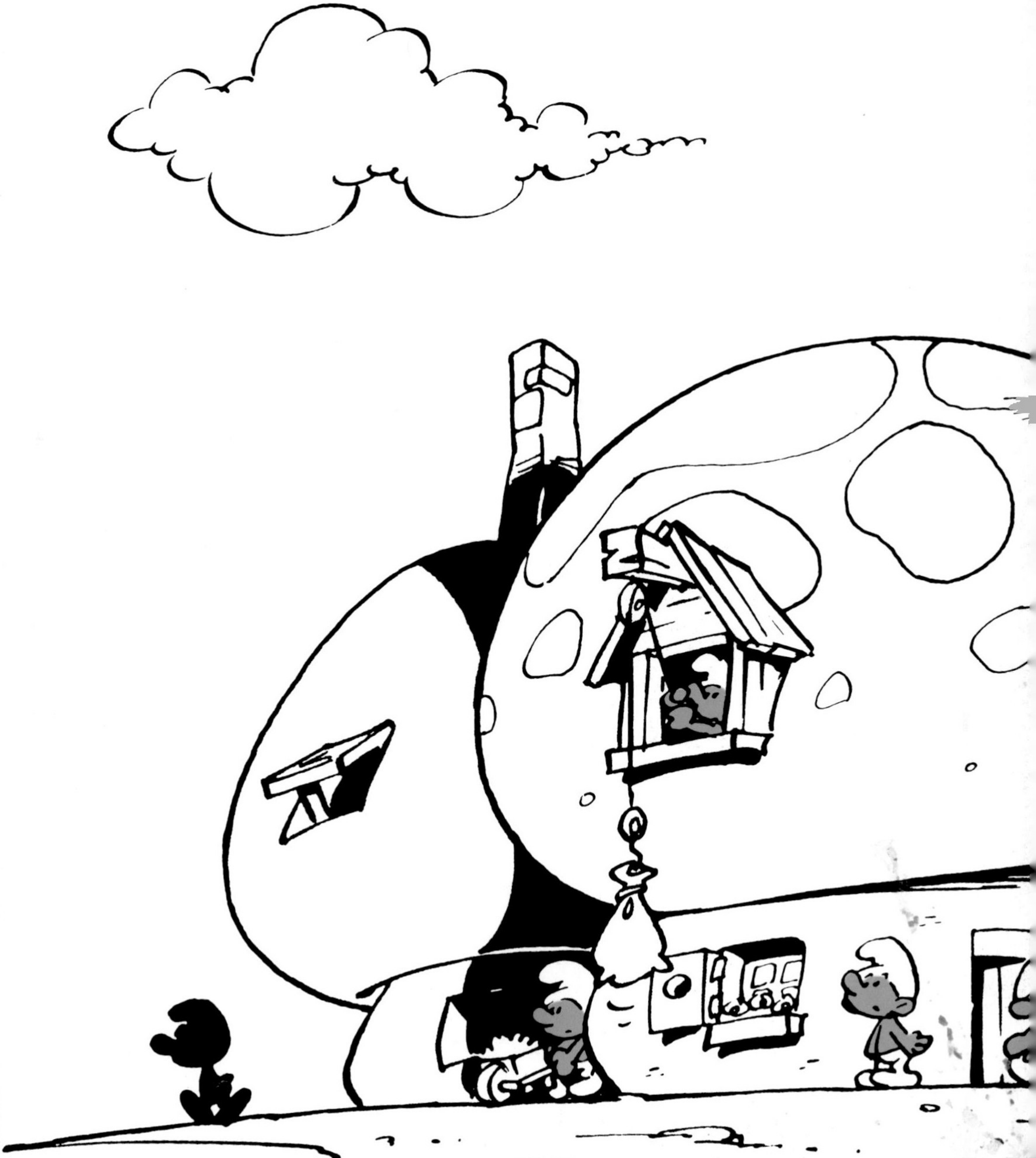

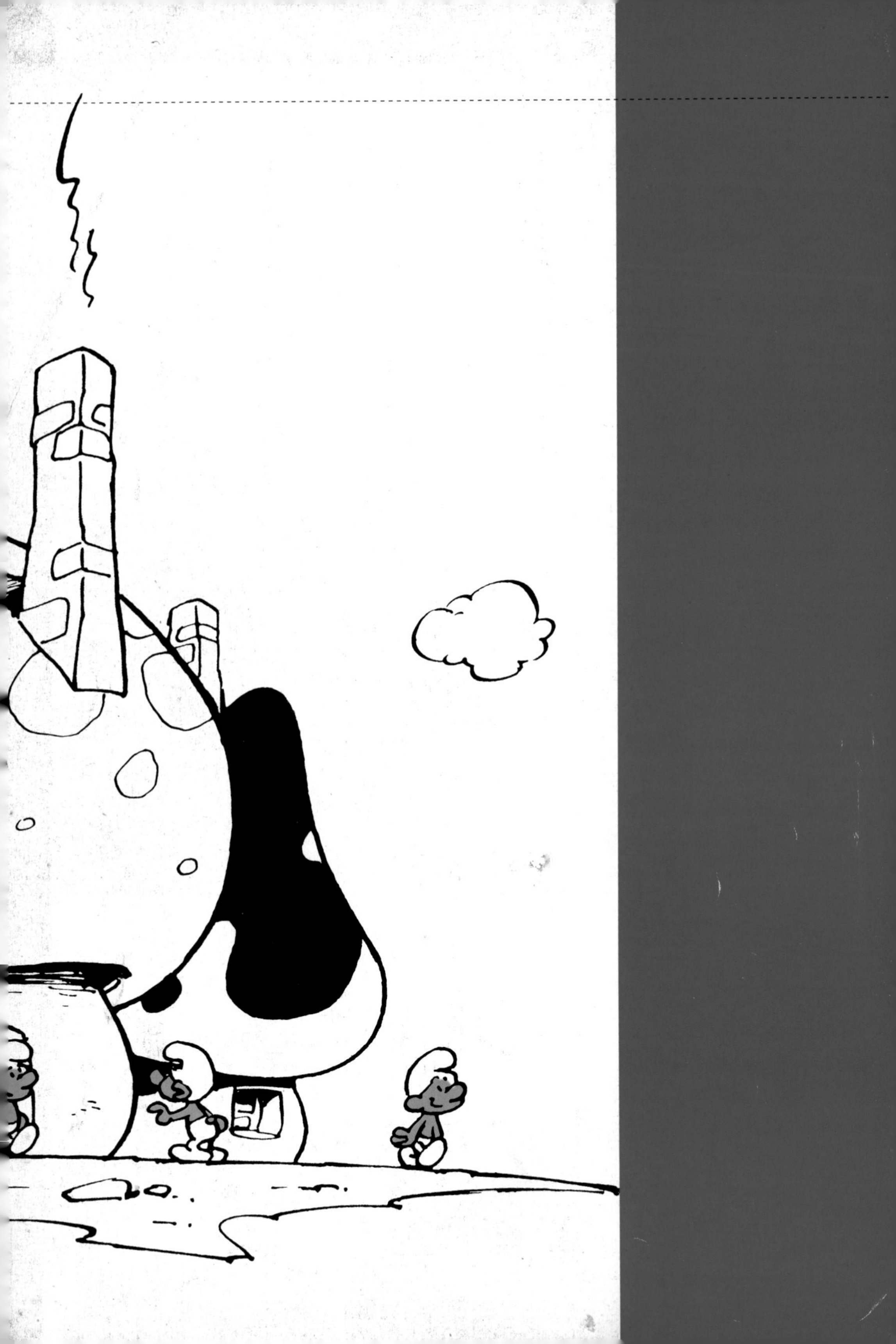

THE PURPLE SMURFS

A SMURFS GRAPHIC NOVEL BY Peyo

PAPERCUTZ™

NEW YORK

SMURFS GRAPHIC NOVELS AVAILABLE FROM PAPERCUTZ™

THE SMURFS graphic novels are available in paperback for $5.99 each and in hardcover for $10.99 each, except for THE SMURFS #21, which is $7.99 in paperback and $12.99 in hardcover, at booksellers everywhere. You can also order online at papercutz.com. Or call 1-800-886-1223, Monday through Friday, 9 – 5 EST. MC, Visa, and AmEx accepted. To order by mail, please add $4.00 for postage and handling for first book ordered, $1.00 for each additional book and make check payable to NBM Publishing. Send to: Papercutz, 160 Broadway, Suite 700, East Wing, New York, NY 10038.

THE SMURFS graphic novels are also available digitally wherever e-books are sold.

PAPERCUTZ.COM

THE PURPLE SMURFS

SMURF™ © Peyo - 2010 - Licensed through Lafig Belgium - www.smurf.com

"The Purple Smurfs"
  BY YVAN DELPORTE AND PEYO

"The Flying Smurf"
  BY YVAN DELPORTE AND PEYO

"The Smurf and his Neighbors"
  © PEYO

Joe Johnson, SMURFLATIONS
Adam Grano, SMURFIC DESIGN
Janice Chiang, LETTERING SMURFETTE
Beth Scorzato, SMURF COORDINATOR
Michael Petranek, ASSOCIATE SMURF
Diego Jourdan, PURPLE SMURFILIZATION
Matt. Murray, SMURF CONSULTANT
Jim Salicrup, SMURF-IN-CHIEF

PAPERBACK EDITION ISBN: 978-1-59707-206-9
HARDCOVER EDITION ISBN: 978-1-59707-207-6

PRINTED IN CHINA JUNE 2016 BY WKT CO. LTD.
3/F PHASE 1 LEADER INDUSTRIAL CENTRE
188 TEXACO ROAD, TSEUN WAN, N.T., HONG KONG

Papercutz books may be purchased for business or promotional use. For information on bulk purchases please contact Macmillan Corporate and Premium Sales Department at (800) 221-7945 x5442.

DISTRIBUTED BY MACMILLAN
EIGHTH PAPERCUTZ PRINTING

THE PURPLE SMURFS

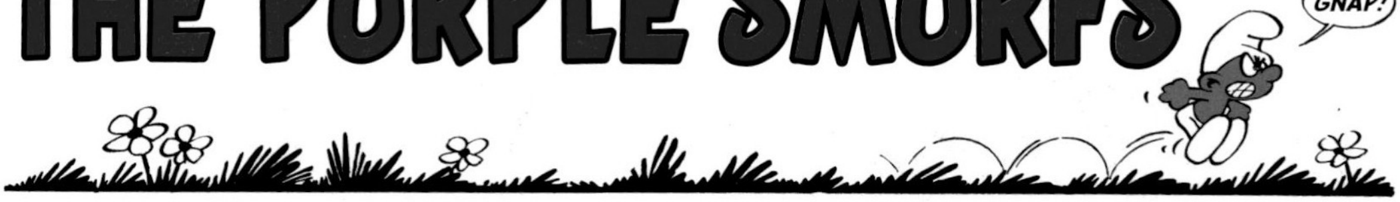

GNAP!

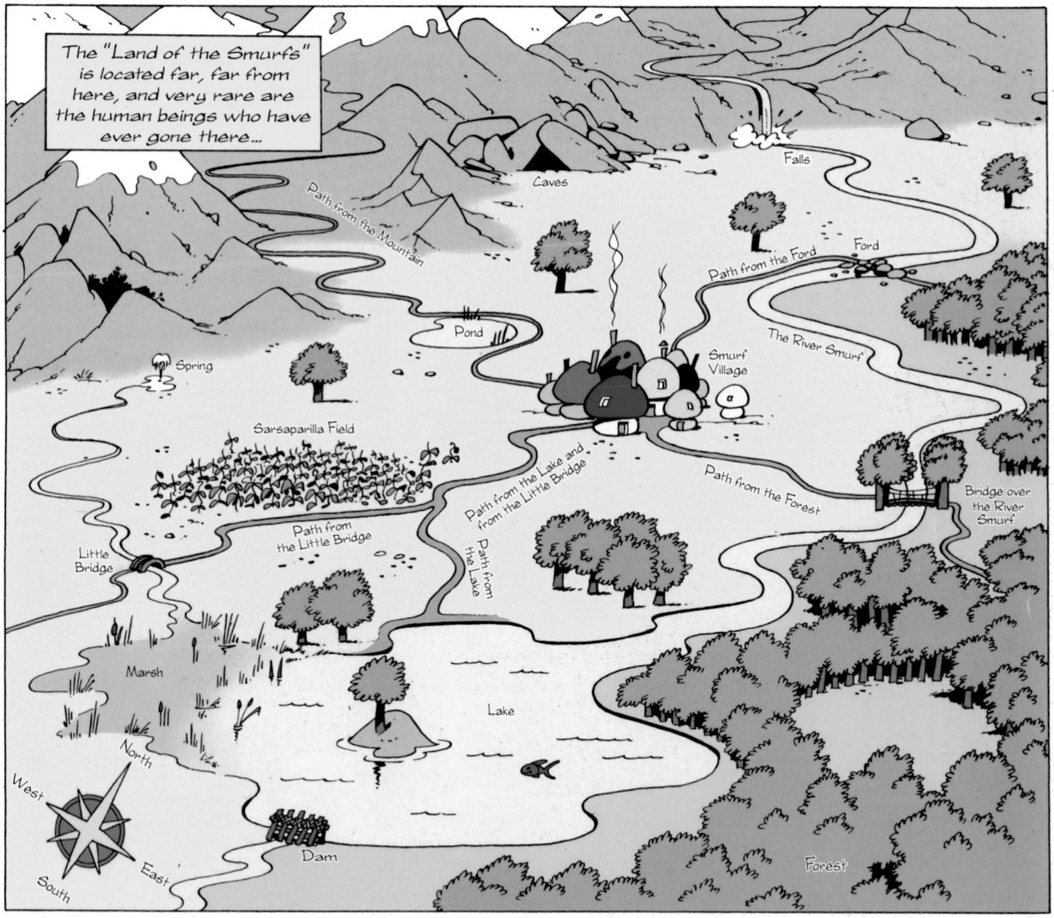

The "Land of the Smurfs" is located far, far from here, and very rare are the human beings who have ever gone there...
Caves
Falls
Path from the Mountain
Ford
Path from the Ford
Pond
The River Smurf
Smurf Village
Spring
Sarsaparilla Field
Path from the Lake and from the Little Bridge
Path from the Forest
Bridge over the River Smurf
Path from the Little Bridge
Little Bridge
Path from the Lake
Marsh
Lake
North
West
East
South
Dam
Forest

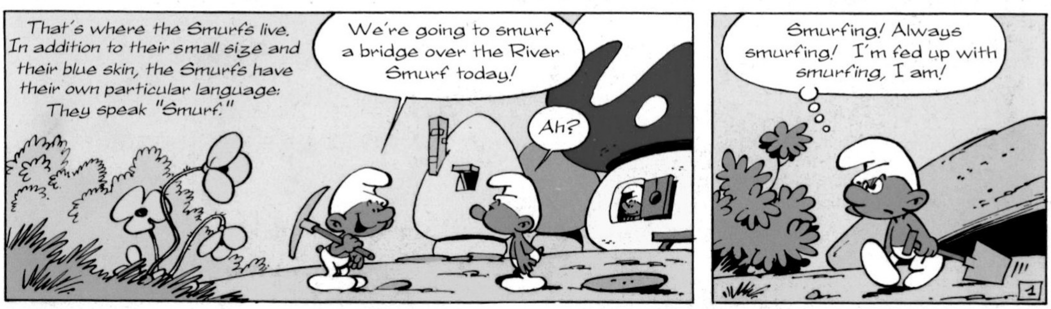

That's where the Smurfs live. In addition to their small size and their blue skin, the Smurfs have their own particular language: They speak "Smurf."
We're going to smurf a bridge over the River Smurf today!
Ah?
Smurfing! Always smurfing! I'm fed up with smurfing, I am!
1

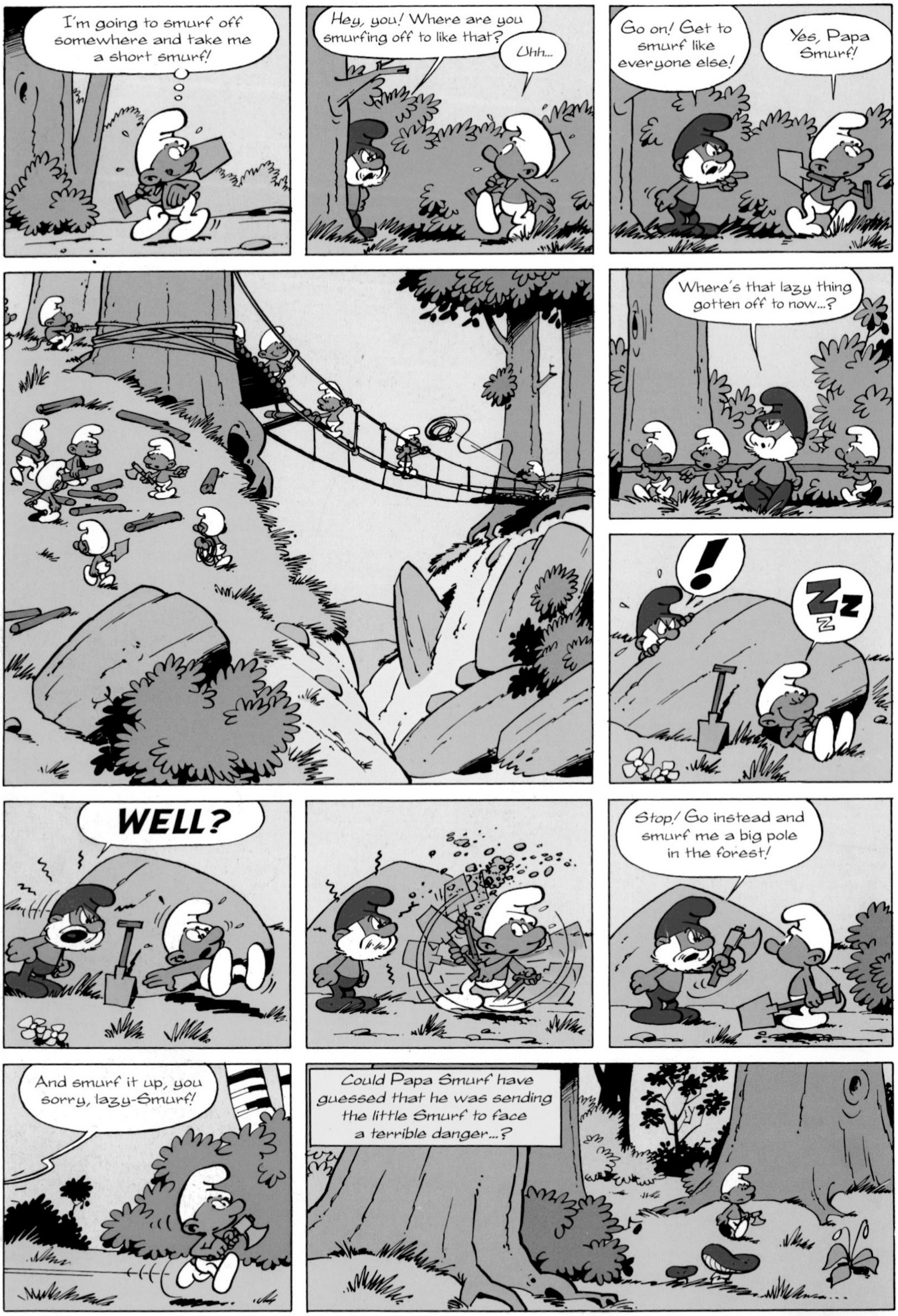

I'm going to smurf off somewhere and take me a short smurf!
Hey, you! Where are you smurfing off to like that?
Uhh...
Go on! Get to smurf like everyone else!
Yes, Papa Smurf!
Where's that lazy thing gotten off to now...?
!
ZZZ
WELL?
Stop! Go instead and smurf me a big pole in the forest!
And smurf it up, you sorry, lazy-Smurf!
Could Papa Smurf have guessed that he was sending the little Smurf to face a terrible danger...?

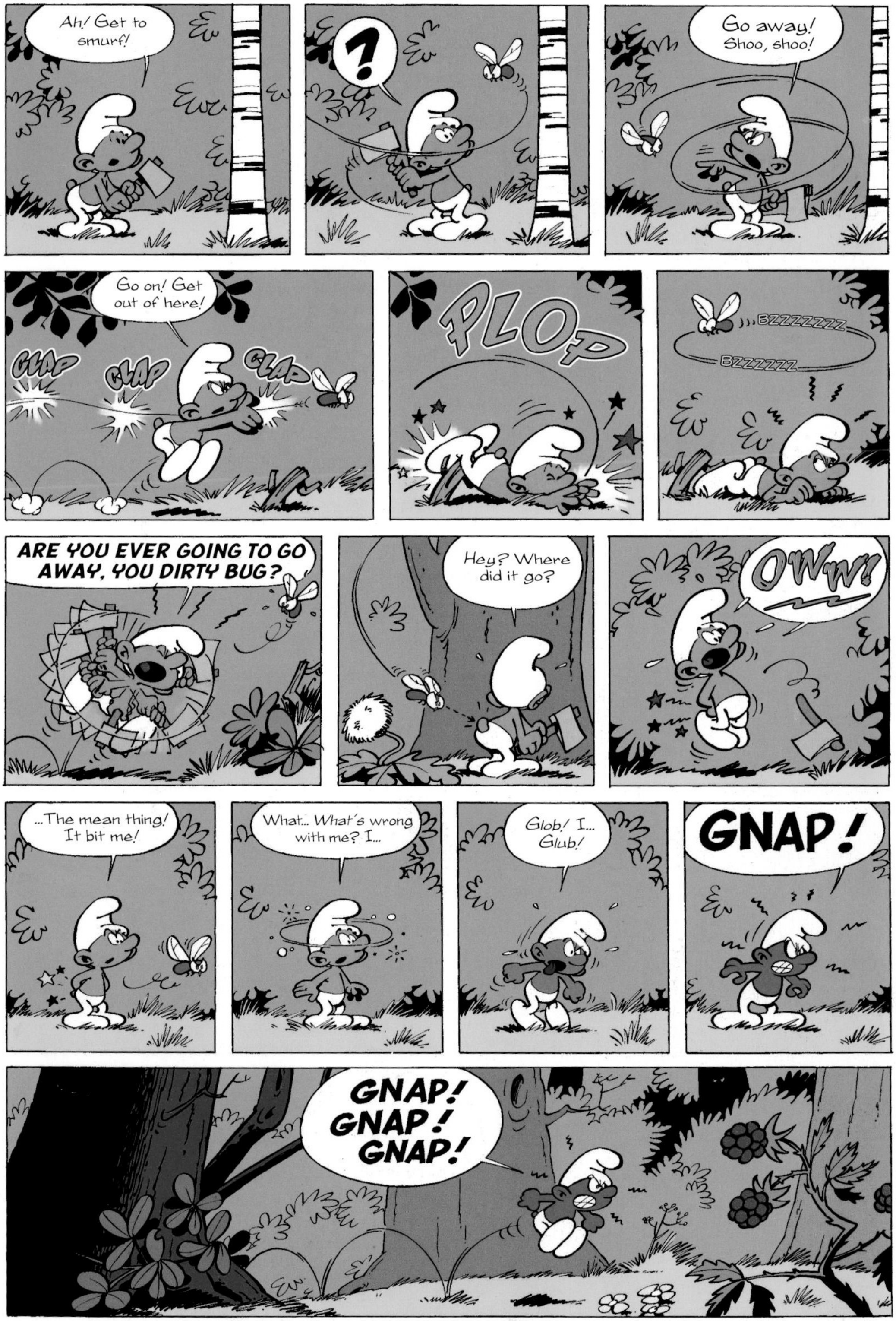

Ah! Get to smurf!
?
Go away! Shoo, shoo!
Go on! Get out of here!
CLAP
CLAP
CLAP
PLOP
BZZZZZZZ
BZZZZZZ
ARE YOU EVER GOING TO GO AWAY, YOU DIRTY BUG?
Hey? Where did it go?
OWW!
...The mean thing! It bit me!
What... What's wrong with me? I...
Glob! I... Glub!
GNAP!
GNAP! GNAP! GNAP!

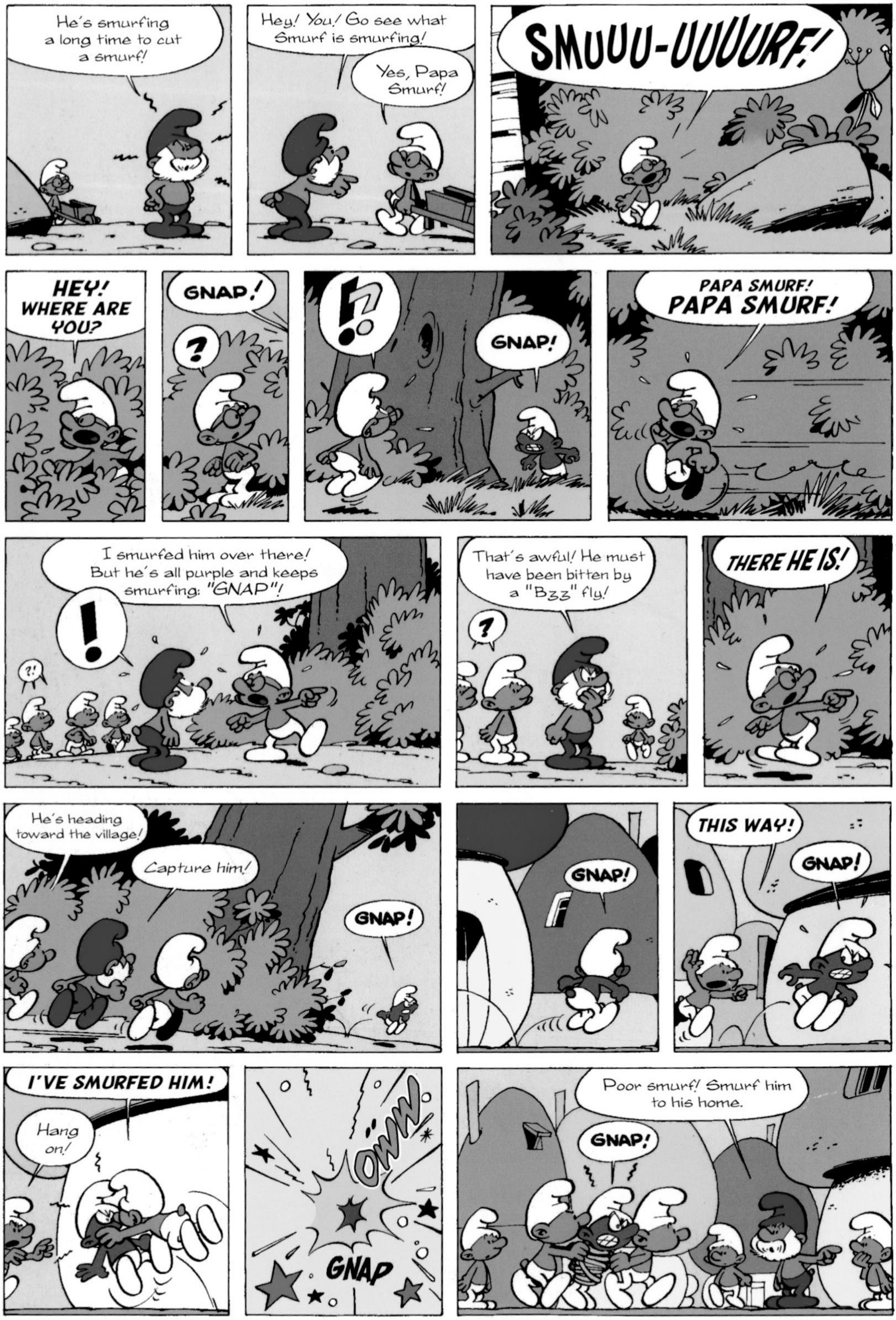
He's smurfing a long time to cut a smurf!
Hey! You! Go see what Smurf is smurfing!
Yes, Papa Smurf!
SMUUU-UUUURF!
HEY! WHERE ARE YOU?
GNAP!
?
!?
GNAP!
PAPA SMURF! PAPA SMURF!
!
?!
I smurfed him over there! But he's all purple and keeps smurfing: "GNAP"!
?
That's awful! He must have been bitten by a "Bzz" fly!
THERE HE IS!
He's heading toward the village!
Capture him!
GNAP!
GNAP!
THIS WAY!
GNAP!
I'VE SMURFED HIM!
Hang on!
OWW
GNAP
Poor smurf! Smurf him to his home.
GNAP!

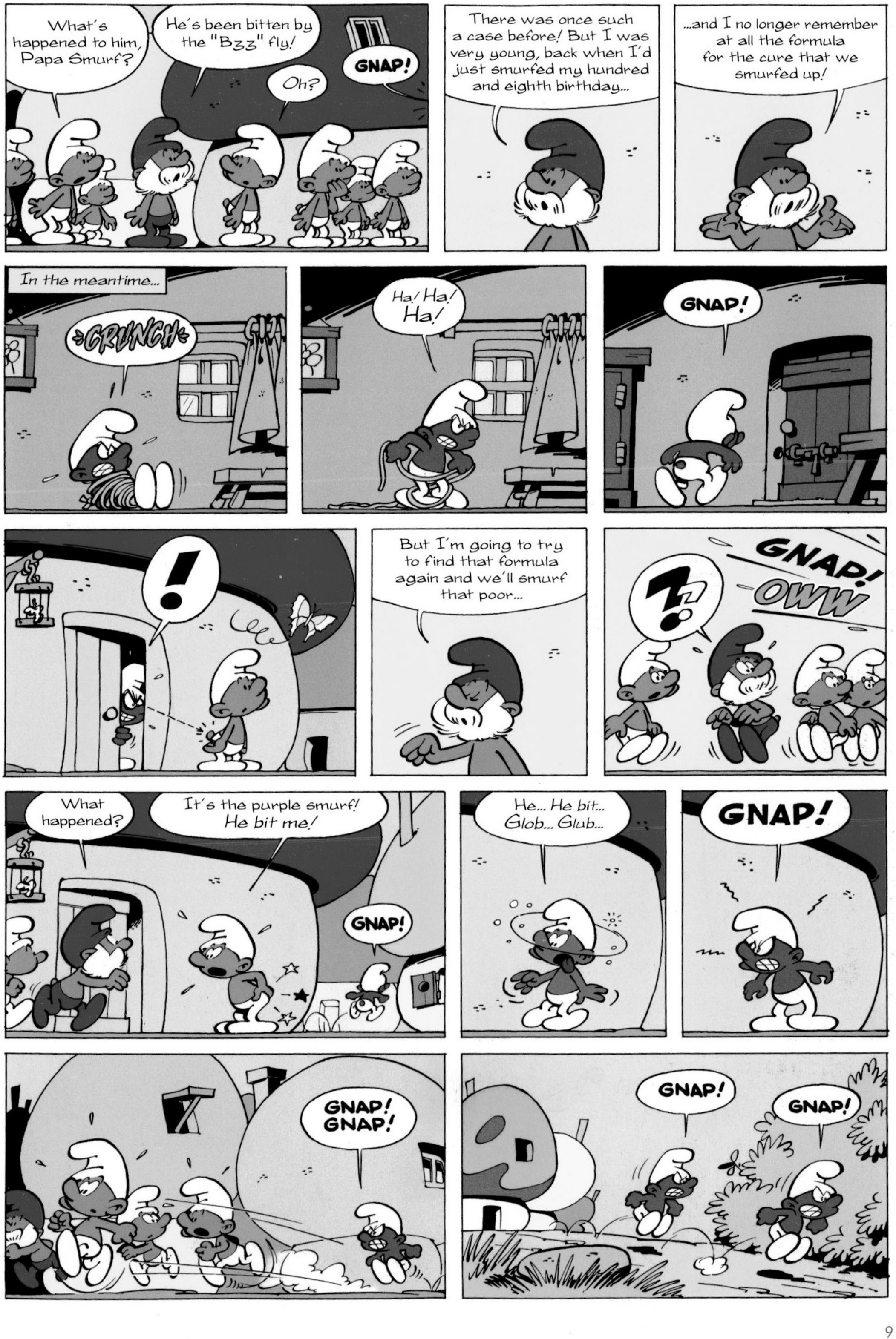
What's happened to him, Papa Smurf?
He's been bitten by the "Bzz" fly!
Oh?
GNAP!
There was once such a case before! But I was very young, back when I'd just smurfed my hundred and eighth birthday...
...and I no longer remember at all the formula for the cure that we smurfed up!
In the meantime...
CRUNCH
Ha! Ha! Ha!
GNAP!
!
But I'm going to try to find that formula again and we'll smurf that poor...
GNAP!
OWW
What happened?
It's the purple smurf! He bit me!
GNAP!
He... He bit... Glob... Glub...
GNAP!
GNAP! GNAP!
GNAP!
GNAP!

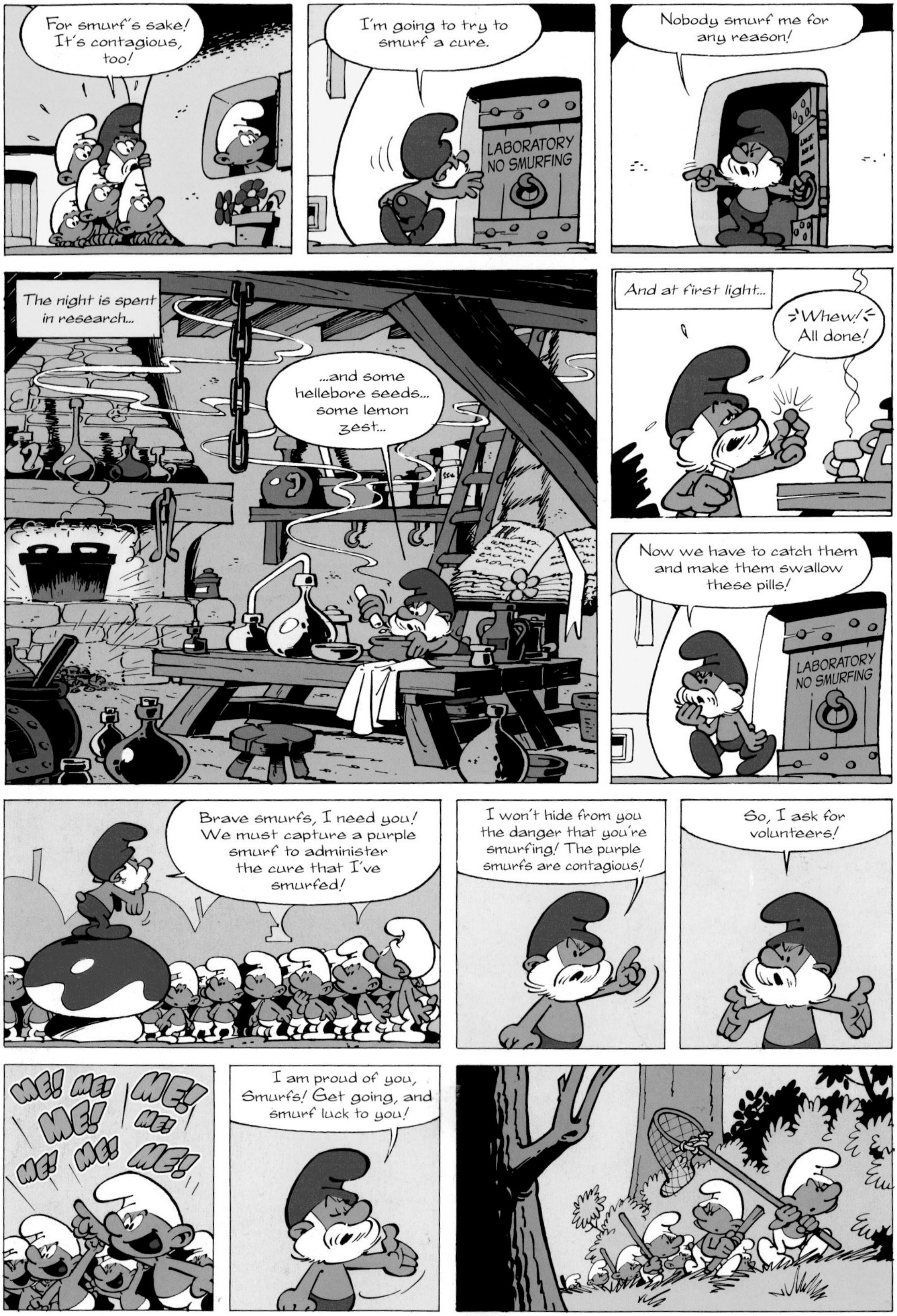
For smurf's sake! It's contagious, too!
I'm going to try to smurf a cure.
LABORATORY NO SMURFING
Nobody smurf me for any reason!
The night is spent in research...
...and some hellebore seeds... some lemon zest...
And at first light...
Whew! All done!
Now we have to catch them and make them swallow these pills!
LABORATORY NO SMURFING
Brave smurfs, I need you! We must capture a purple smurf to administer the cure that I've smurfed!
I won't hide from you the danger that you're smurfing! The purple smurfs are contagious!
So, I ask for volunteers!
ME! ME! ME! ME! ME! ME! ME! ME!
I am proud of you, Smurfs! Get going, and smurf luck to you!

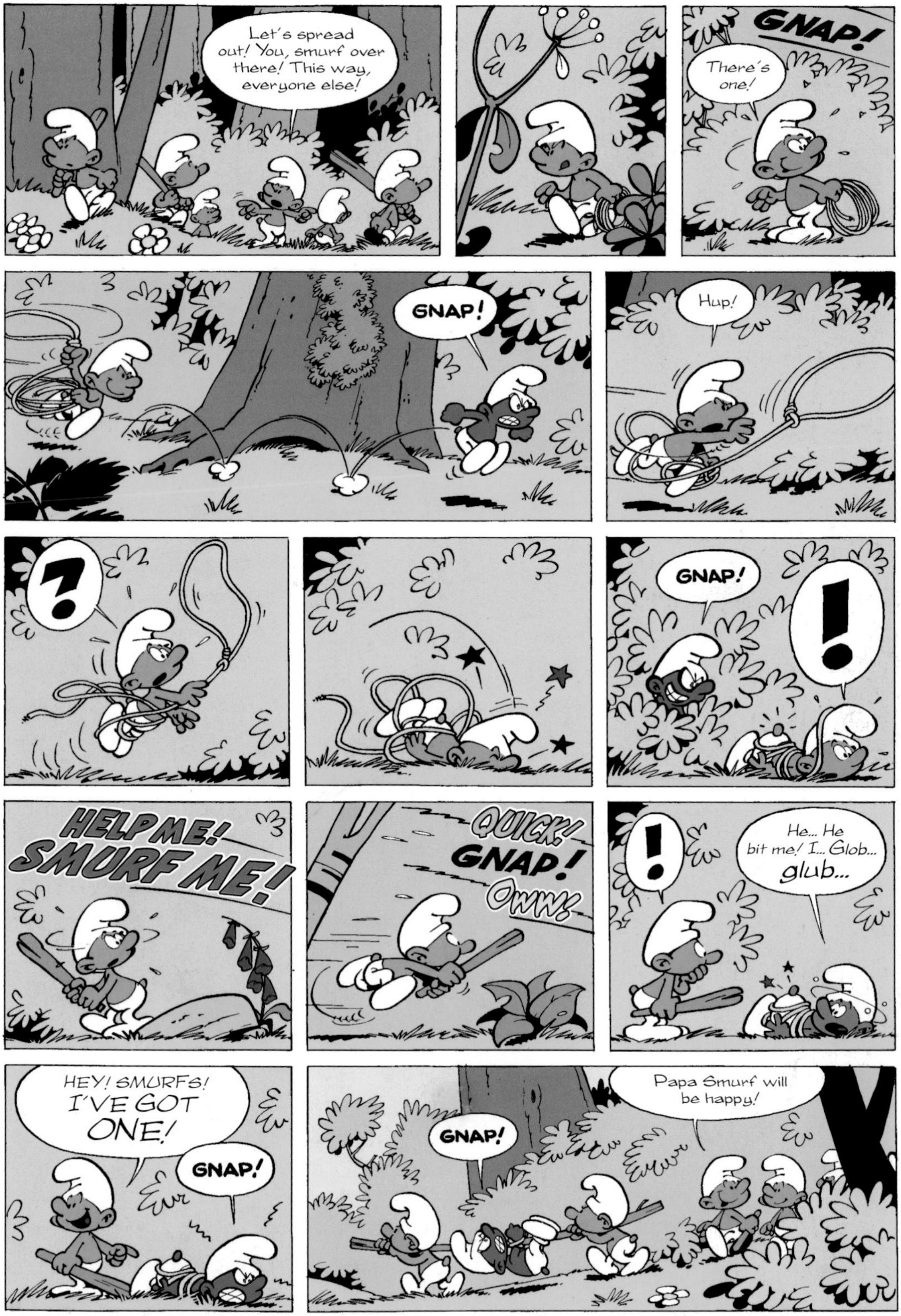
Let's spread out! You, smurf over there! This way, everyone else!
GNAP!
There's one!
GNAP!
Hup!
?
GNAP!
!
HELP ME! SMURF ME!
QUICK!
GNAP!
OWW!
!
He... He bit me! I... Glob... glub...
HEY! SMURFS! I'VE GOT ONE!
GNAP!
GNAP!
Papa Smurf will be happy!

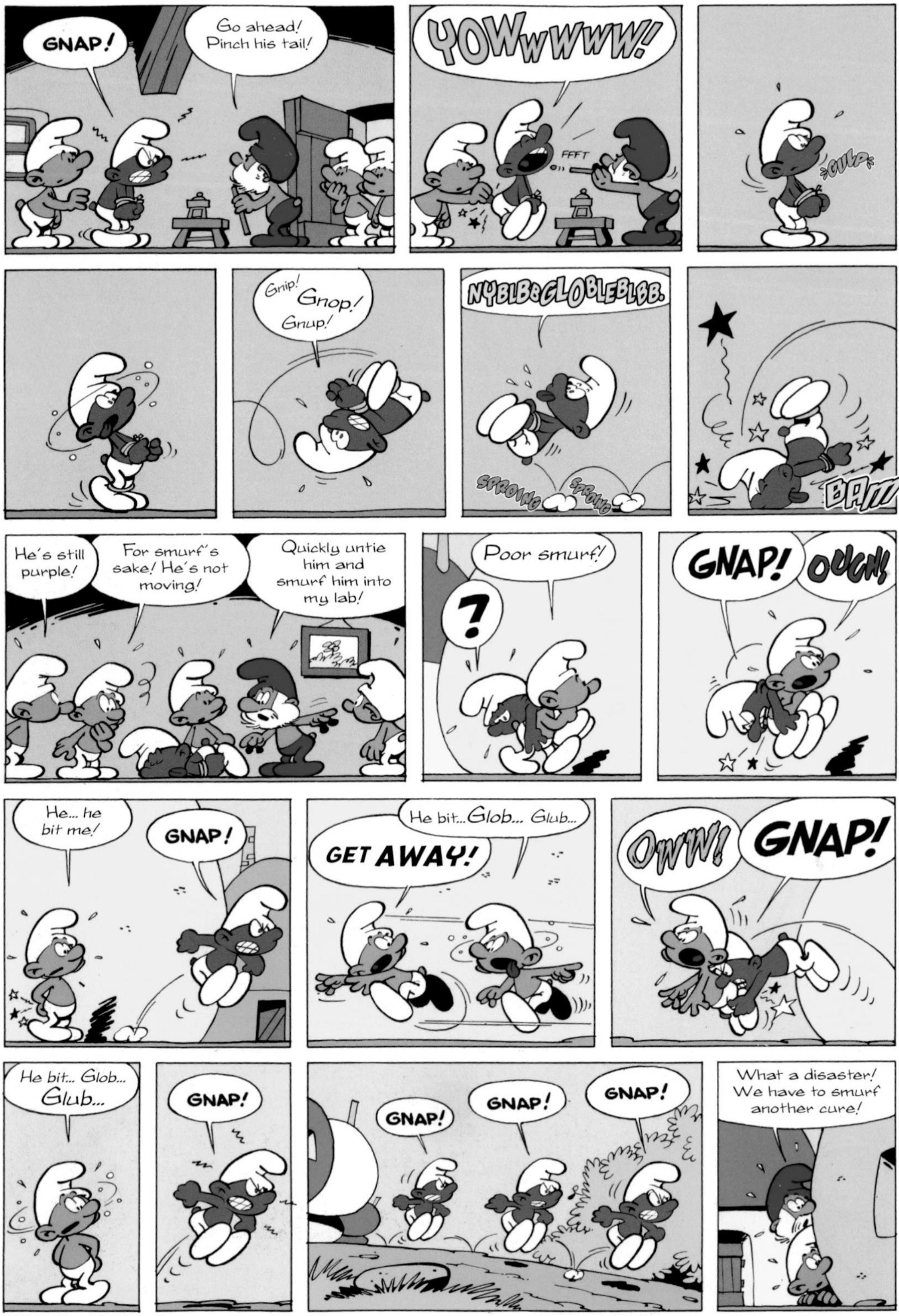
GNAP!
Go ahead! Pinch his tail!
YOWWWWW!
FFFT
GULP
Grip! Gnop! Gnup!
NYBLBBGLOBLEBLBB.
SPROING
SPROING
BAM
He's still purple!
For smurf's sake! He's not moving!
Quickly untie him and smurf him into my lab!
Poor smurf!
?
GNAP!
OUCH!
He... he bit me!
GNAP!
GET AWAY!
He bit... Glob... Glub...
OWW!
GNAP!
He bit... Glob... Glub...
GNAP!
GNAP!
GNAP!
GNAP!
What a disaster! We have to smurf another cure!

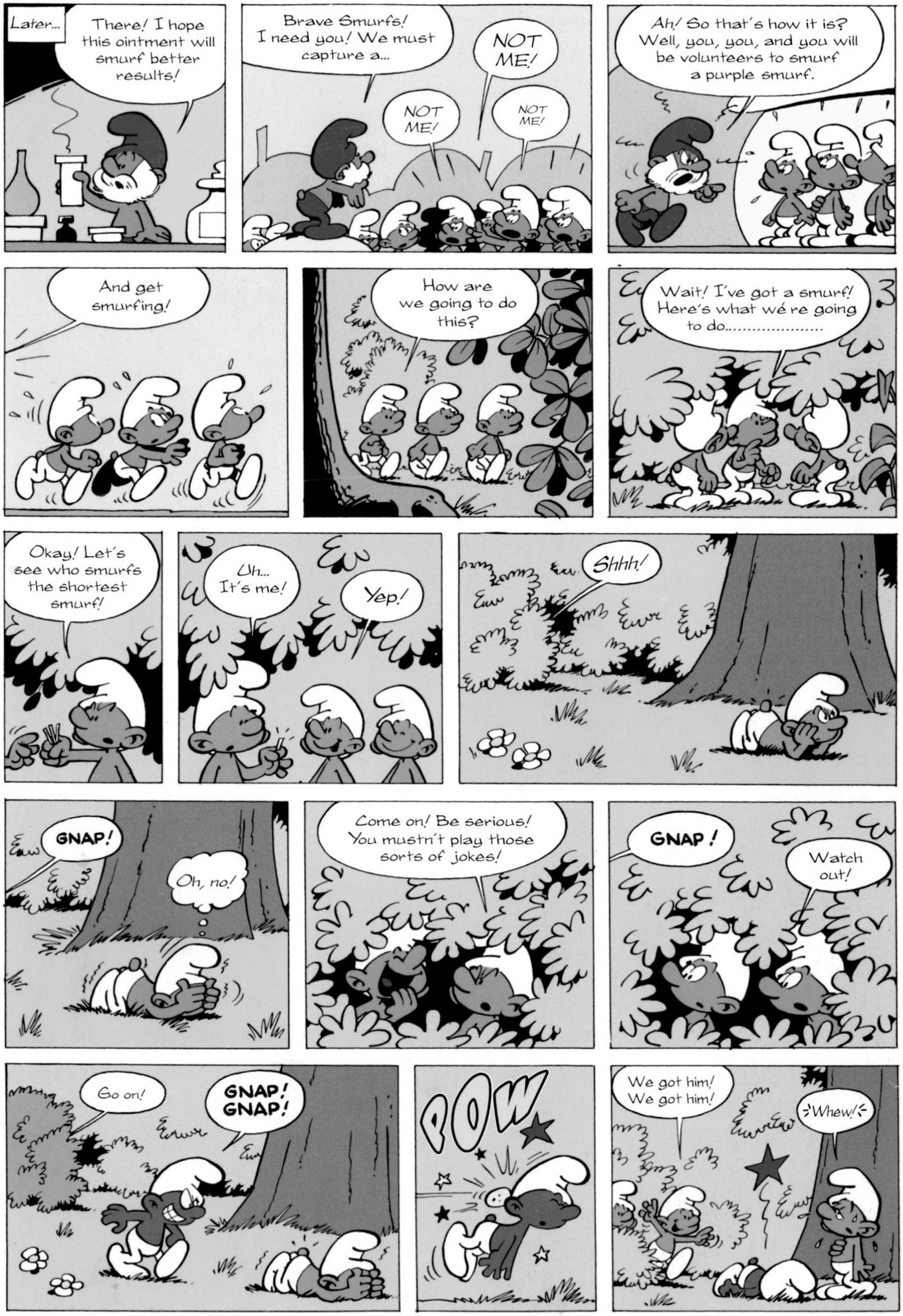

Later...
There! I hope this ointment will smurf better results!
Brave Smurfs! I need you! We must capture a...
NOT ME!
NOT ME!
NOT ME!
Ah! So that's how it is? Well, you, you, and you will be volunteers to smurf a purple smurf.
And get smurfing!
How are we going to do this?
Wait! I've got a smurf! Here's what wé re going to do....................
Okay! Let's see who smurfs the shortest smurf!
Uh... It's me!
Yep!
Shhh!
GNAP!
Oh, no!
Come on! Be serious! You mustn't play those sorts of jokes!
GNAP!
Watch out!
Go on!
GNAP! GNAP!
POW
We got him! We got him!
Whew!

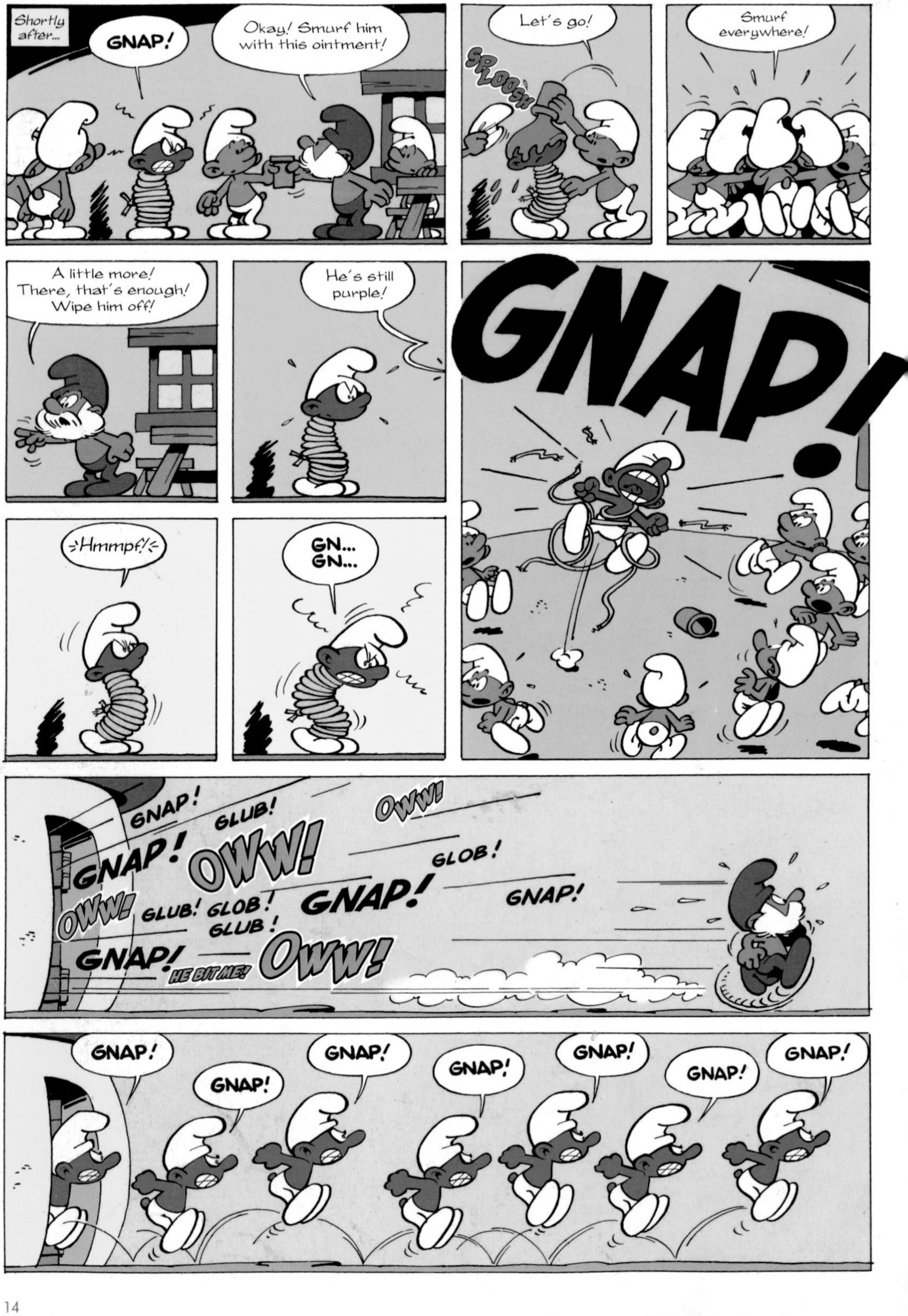

Shortly after...
GNAP!
Okay! Smurf him with this ointment!
SPLOOSH
Let's go!
Smurf everywhere!
A little more! There, that's enough! Wipe him off!
He's still purple!
GNAP!
Hmmpf!
GN... GN...
GNAP!
GLUB!
OWW!
GNAP!
OWW!
GLOB!
OWW!
GLUB! GLOB!
GNAP!
GNAP!
GLUB!
GNAP!
HE BIT ME!
OWW!
GNAP!
GNAP!
GNAP!
GNAP!
GNAP!
GNAP!
GNAP!

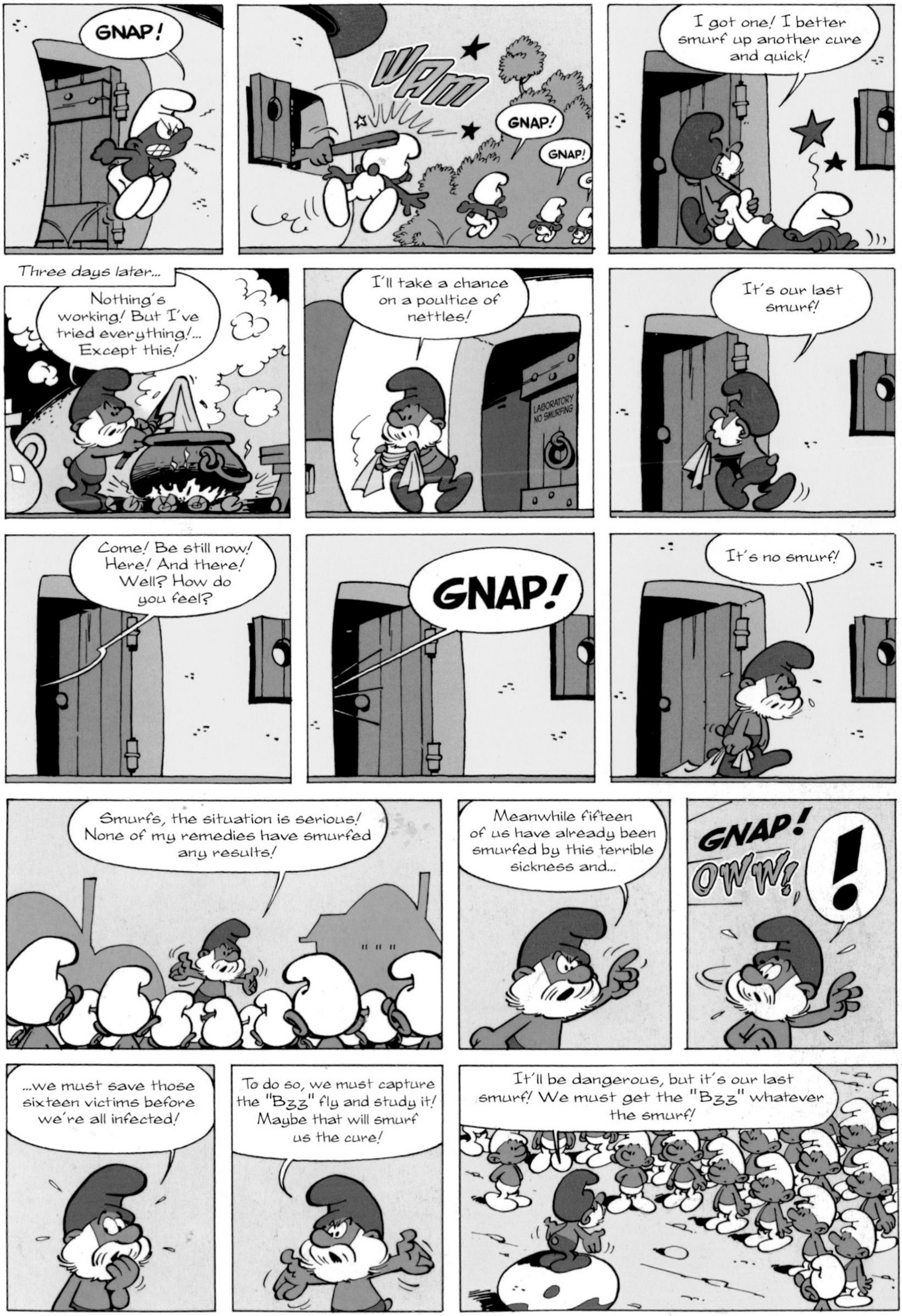
GNAP!
WAM
GNAP!
GNAP!
I got one! I better smurf up another cure and quick!
Three days later...
Nothing's working! But I've tried everything!... Except this!
I'll take a chance on a poultice of nettles!
LABORATORY NO SMURFING
It's our last smurf!
Come! Be still now! Here! And there! Well? How do you feel?
GNAP!
It's no smurf!
Smurfs, the situation is serious! None of my remedies have smurfed any results!
Meanwhile fifteen of us have already been smurfed by this terrible sickness and...
GNAP!
OWW!
!
...we must save those sixteen victims before we're all infected!
To do so, we must capture the "Bzz" fly and study it! Maybe that will smurf us the cure!
It'll be dangerous, but it's our last smurf! We must get the "Bzz" whatever the smurf!

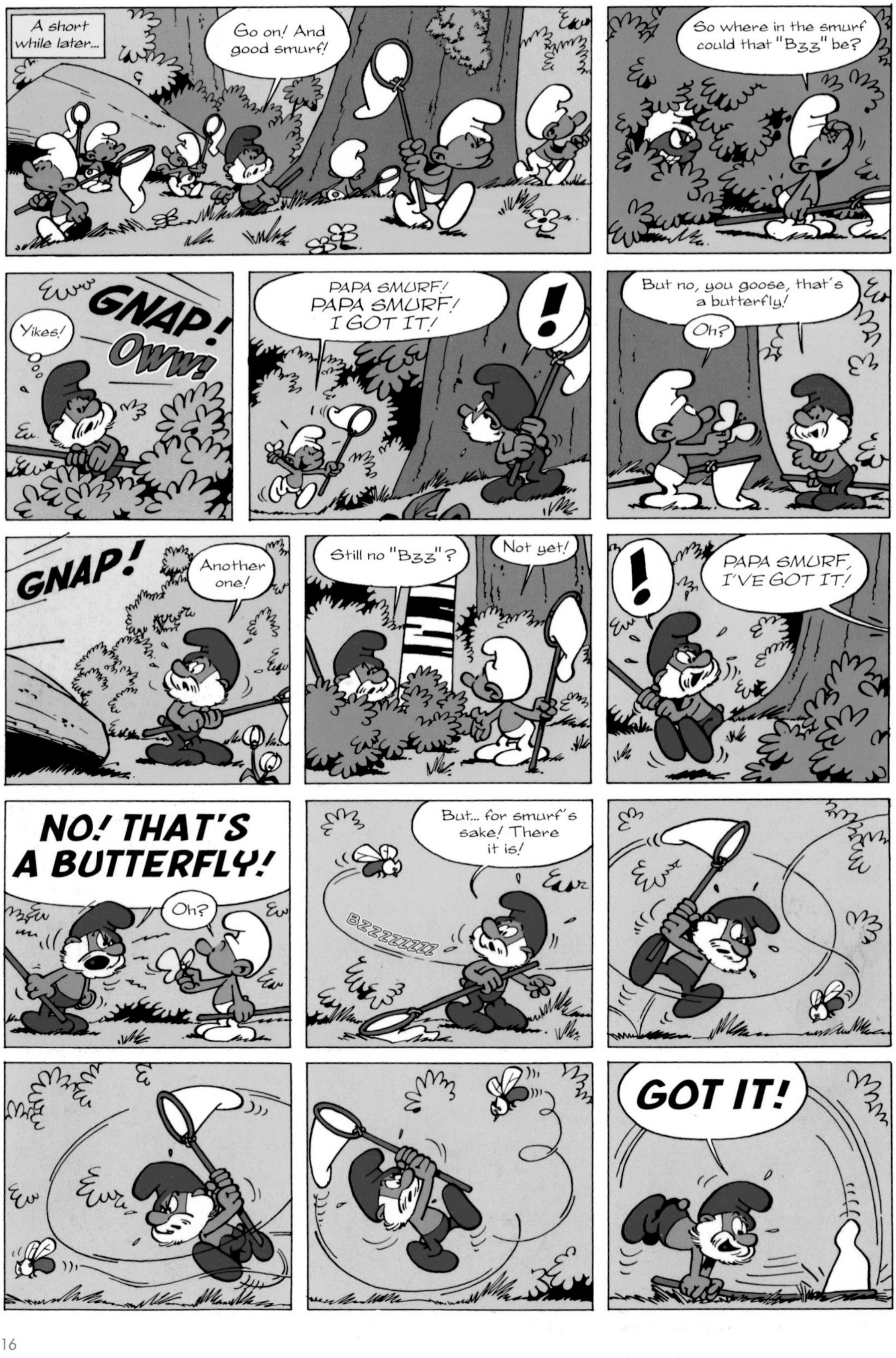
A short while later...
Go on! And good smurf!
So where in the smurf could that "Bzz" be?
Yikes!
GNAP!
OWW!
PAPA SMURF! PAPA SMURF! I GOT IT!
!
But no, you goose, that's a butterfly!
Oh?
GNAP!
Another one!
Still no "Bzz"?
Not yet!
!
PAPA SMURF, I'VE GOT IT!
NO! THAT'S A BUTTERFLY!
Oh?
But... for smurf's sake! There it is!
BZZZZZZZZ
GOT IT!

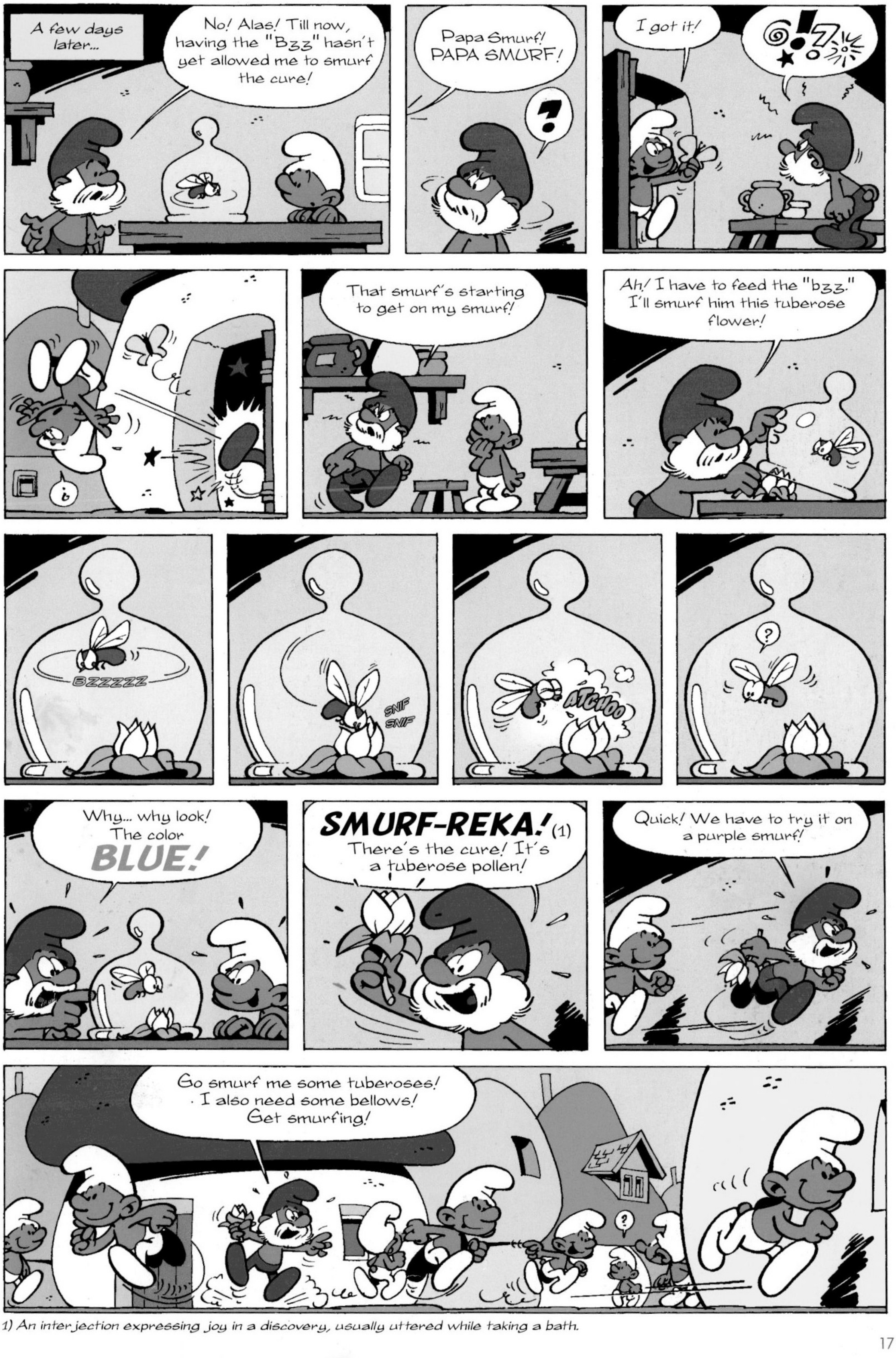
A few days later...
No! Alas! Till now, having the "Bzz" hasn't yet allowed me to smurf the cure!
Papa Smurf! PAPA SMURF!
?
I got it!
That smurf's starting to get on my smurf!
Ah! I have to feed the "bzz." I'll smurf him this tuberose flower!
BZZZZZ
SNIF SNIF
ATCHOO
?
Why... why look! The color BLUE!
SMURF-REKA! (1) There's the cure! It's a tuberose pollen!
Quick! We have to try it on a purple smurf!
Go smurf me some tuberoses! I also need some bellows! Get smurfing!
?

1) An interjection expressing joy in a discovery, usually uttered while taking a bath.

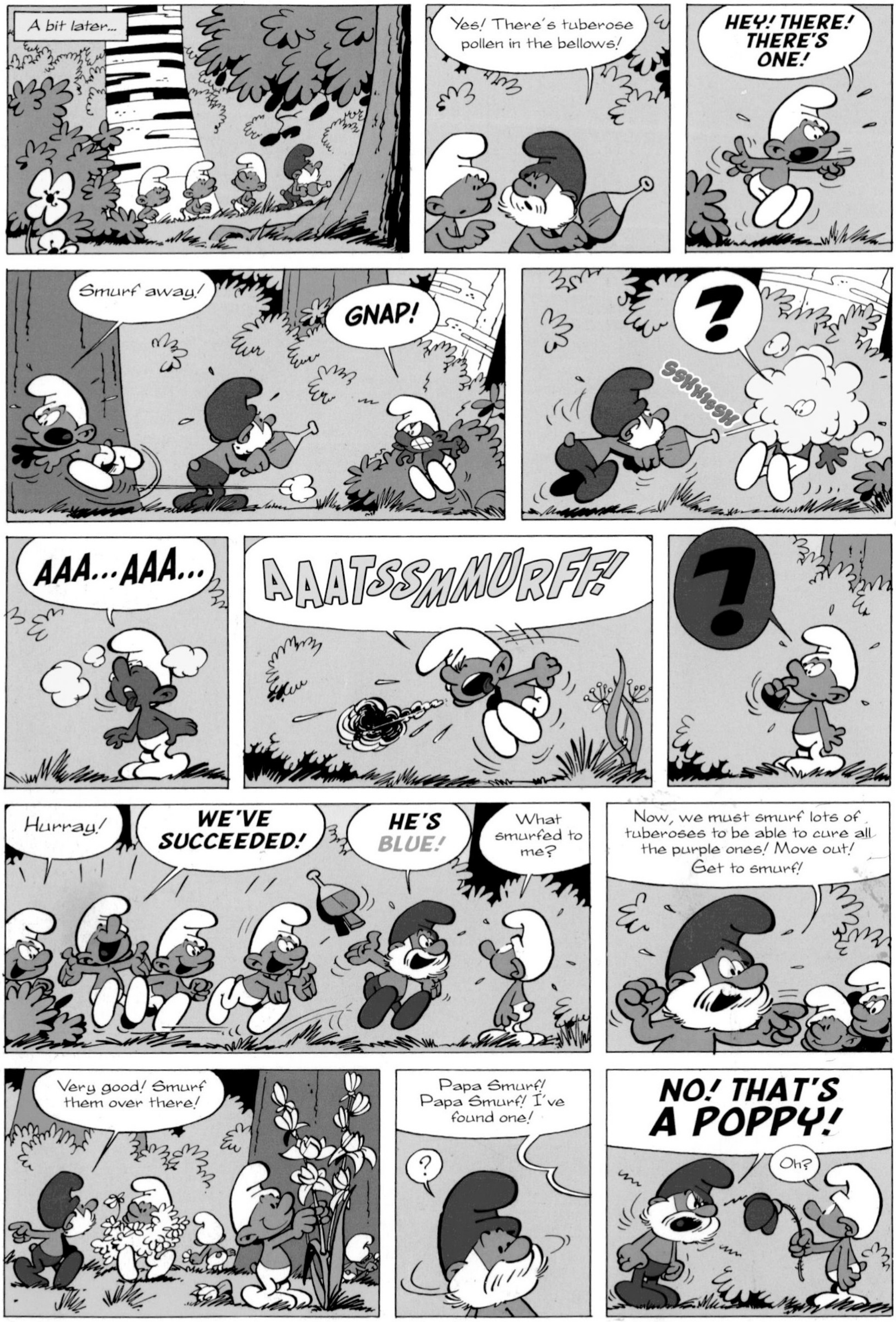
A bit later...
Yes! There's tuberose pollen in the bellows!
HEY! THERE! THERE'S ONE!
Smurf away!
GNAP!
?
AAA... AAA...
AAATSSMMURFF!
?
Hurray!
WE'VE SUCCEEDED!
HE'S BLUE!
What smurfed to me?
Now, we must smurf lots of tuberoses to be able to cure all the purple ones! Move out! Get to smurf!
Very good! Smurf them over there!
Papa Smurf! Papa Smurf! I've found one!
?
NO! THAT'S A POPPY!
Oh?

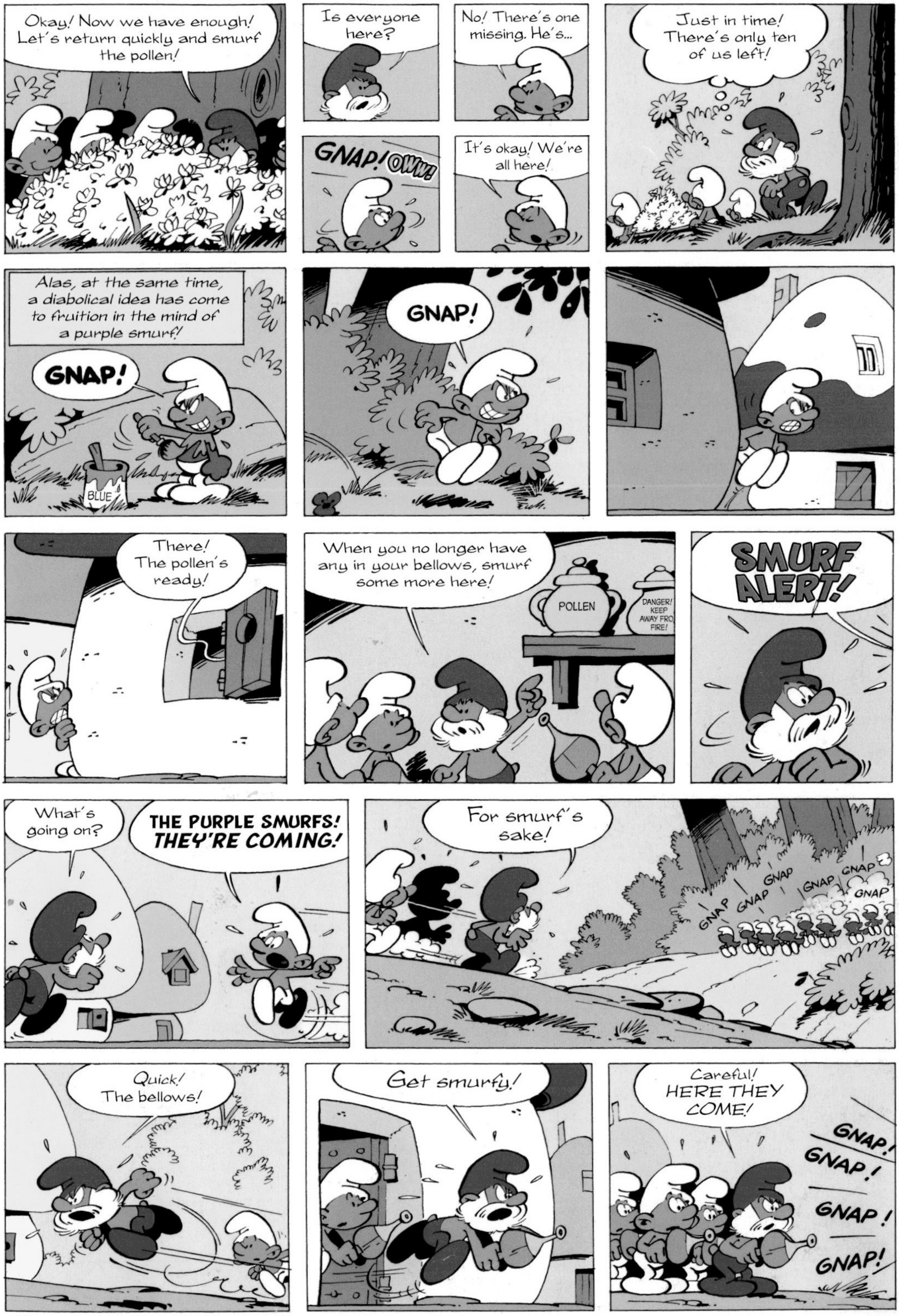

Okay! Now we have enough! Let's return quickly and smurf the pollen!
Is everyone here?
No! There's one missing. He's...
GNAP! OWW!
It's okay! We're all here!
Just in time! There's only ten of us left!
Alas, at the same time, a diabolical idea has come to fruition in the mind of a purple smurf!
GNAP!
BLUE
GNAP!
There! The pollen's ready!
When you no longer have any in your bellows, smurf some more here!
POLLEN
DANGER! KEEP AWAY FRO FIRE!
SMURF ALERT!
What's going on?
THE PURPLE SMURFS! THEY'RE COMING!
For smurf's sake!
GNAP GNAP GNAP GNAP GNAP GNAP GNAP
Quick! The bellows!
Get smurfy!
Careful! HERE THEY COME!
GNAP! GNAP! GNAP! GNAP!

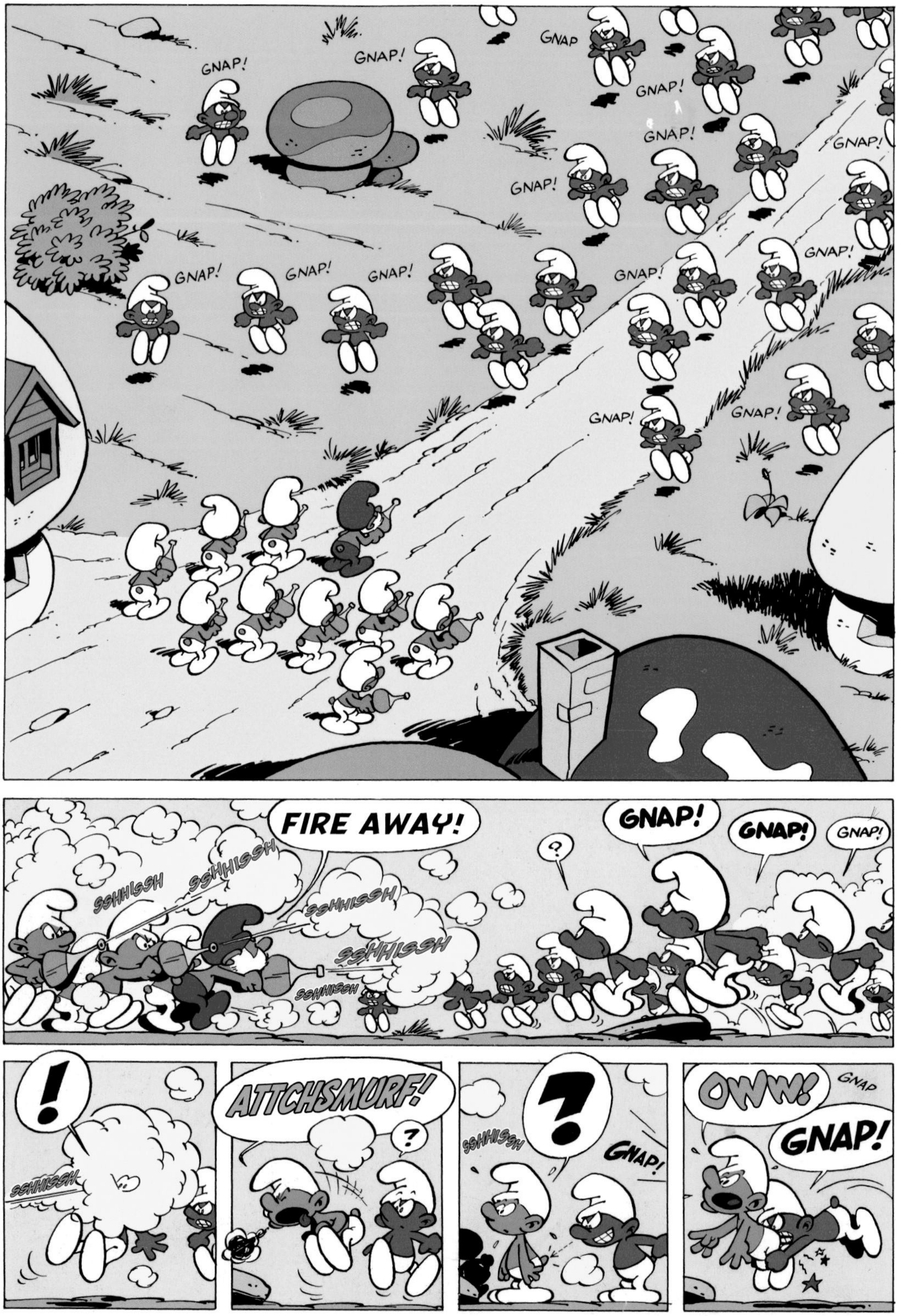
GNAP!
GNAP!
GNAP
GNAP!
GNAP!
GNAP!
GNAP!
GNAP!
GNAP!
GNAP!
GNAP!
GNAP!
GNAP!
GNAP!
GNAP!
FIRE AWAY!
SSHHISSH
SSHHISSH
SSHHISSH
SSHHISSH
SSHHISSH
?
GNAP!
GNAP!
GNAP!
!
SSHHISSH
ATTCHSMURF!
?
?
SSHHISSH
GNAP!
OWW!
GNAP
GNAP!

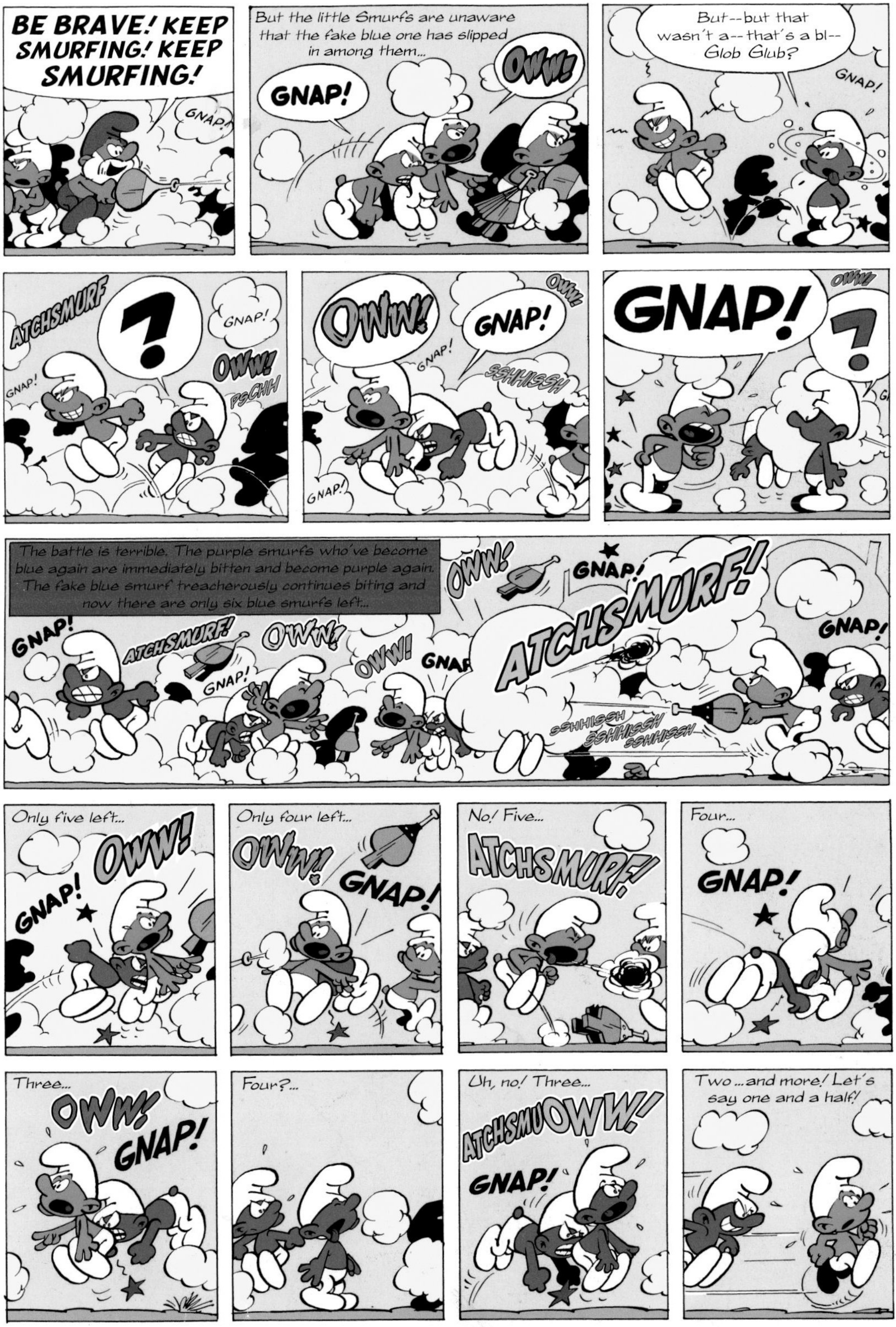
BE BRAVE! KEEP SMURFING! KEEP SMURFING!
GNAP!
But the little Smurfs are unaware that the fake blue one has slipped in among them...
GNAP!
OWW!
But--but that wasn't a--that's a bl-- Glob Glub?
GNAP!
ATCHSMURF
?
GNAP!
GNAP!
OWW!
PSCHH
OWW!
OWW!
GNAP!
GNAP!
SSHHISSH
GNAP!
GNAP!
OWW!
?
The battle is terrible. The purple smurfs who've become blue again are immediately bitten and become purple again. The fake blue smurf treacherously continues biting and now there are only six blue smurfs left...
OWW!
GNAP!
ATCHSMURF!
GNAP!
ATCHSMURF!
OWW!
OWW!
GNAP!
GNAP!
SSHHISSH
SSHHISSH
SSHHISSH
Only five left...
GNAP!
OWW!
Only four left...
OWW!
GNAP!
No! Five...
ATCHSMURF!
Four...
GNAP!
Three...
OWW!
GNAP!
Four?...
Uh, no! Three...
ATCHSMUOWW!
GNAP!
Two ...and more! Let's say one and a half!

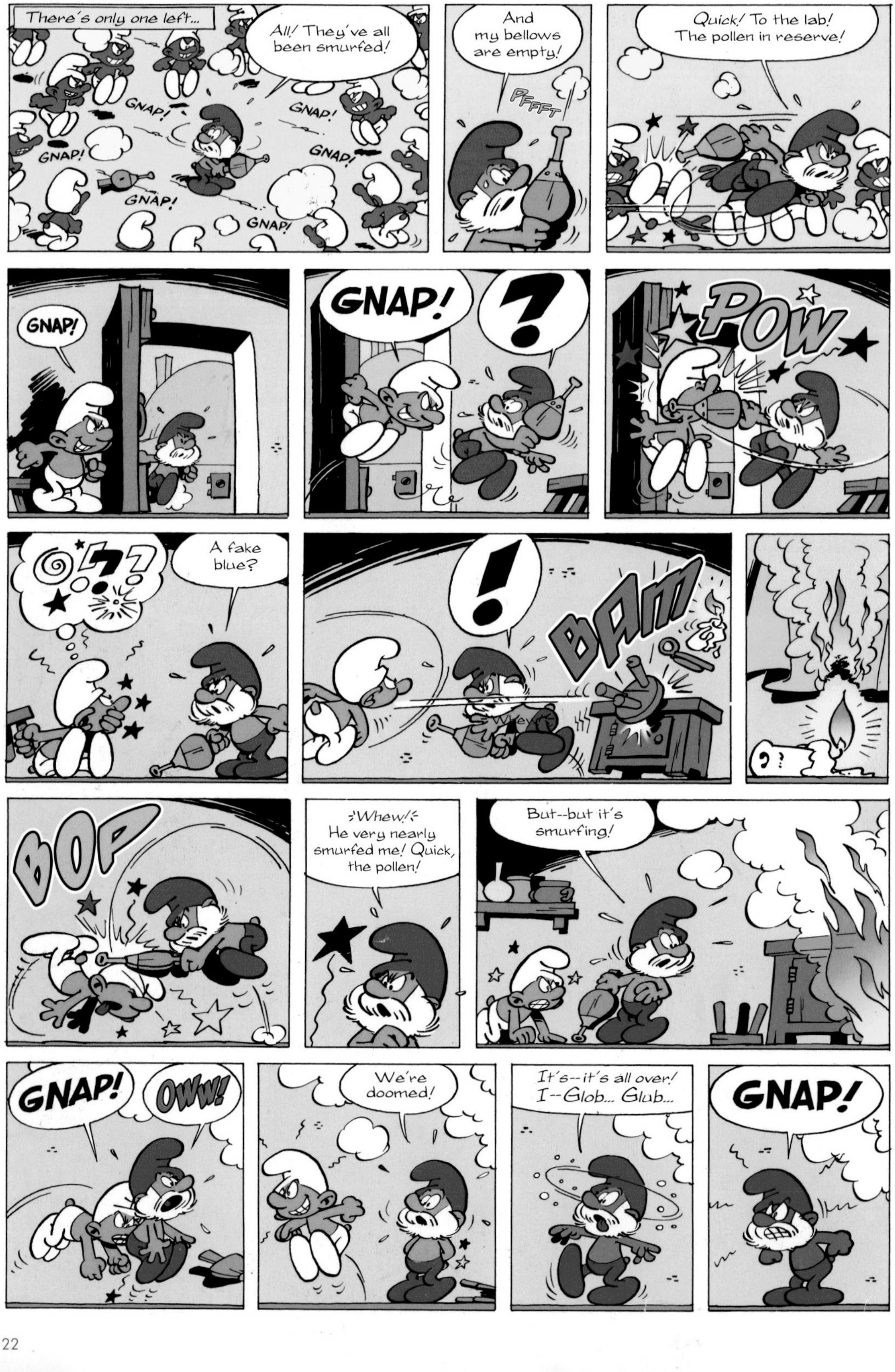
There's only one left...
All! They've all been smurfed!
GNAP!
GNAP!
GNAP!
GNAP!
GNAP!
GNAP!
And my bellows are empty!
PFFFT
Quick! To the lab! The pollen in reserve!
GNAP!
GNAP!
?
POW
A fake blue?
!
BAM
Whew!
BOP
Whew! He very nearly smurfed me! Quick, the pollen!
But--but it's smurfing!
GNAP!
OWW!
We're doomed!
It's--it's all over! I--Glob... Glub...
GNAP!

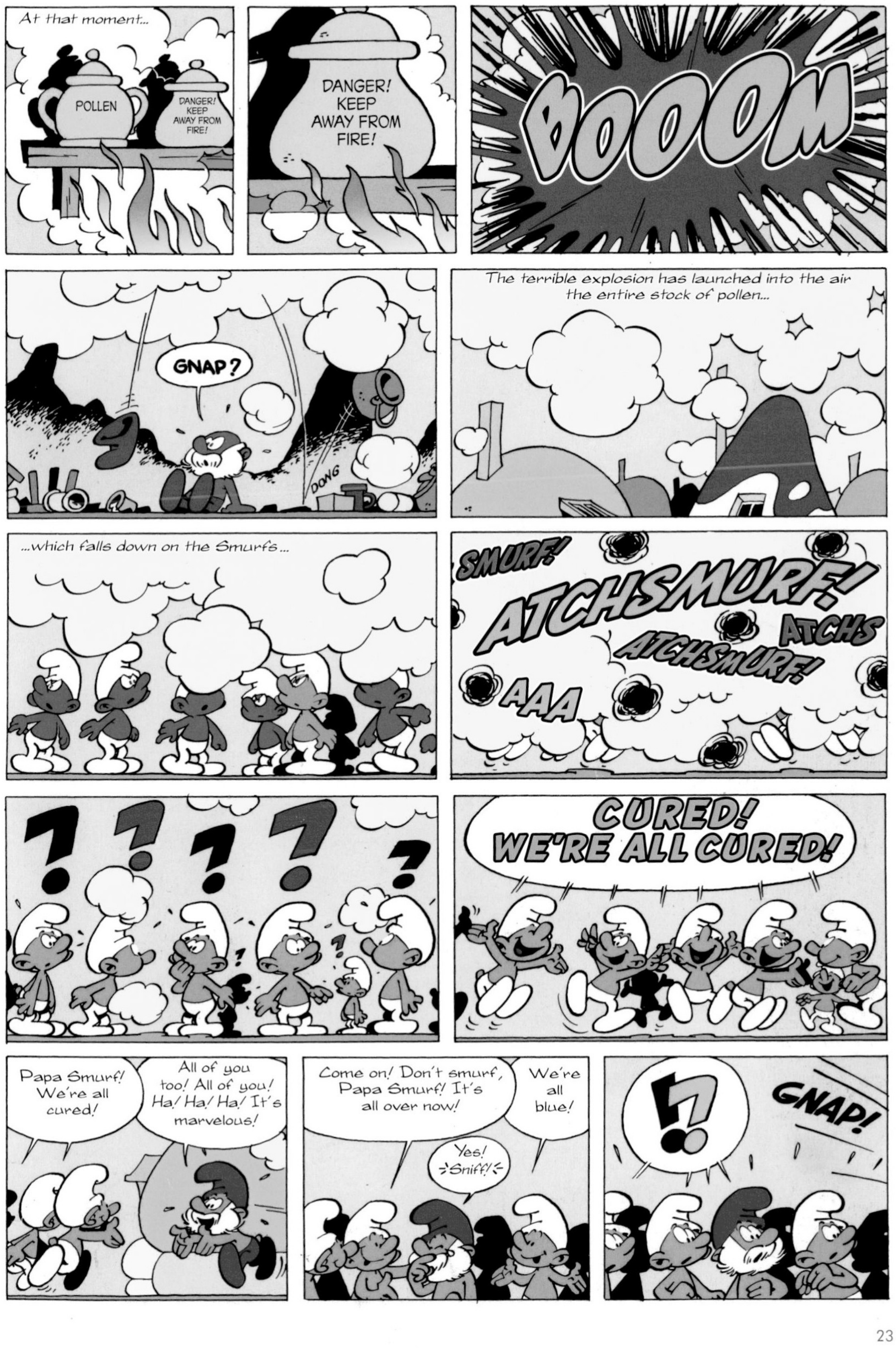
At that moment...
POLLEN
DANGER! KEEP AWAY FROM FIRE!
DANGER! KEEP AWAY FROM FIRE!
BOOOM
GNAP?
DONG
The terrible explosion has launched into the air the entire stock of pollen...
...which falls down on the Smurfs...
SMURF!
ATCHSMURF!
ATCHS
ATCHSMURF!
AAA
CURED! WE'RE ALL CURED!
Papa Smurf! We're all cured!
All of you too! All of you! Ha! Ha! Ha! It's marvelous!
Come on! Don't smurf, Papa Smurf! It's all over now!
We're all blue!
Yes! Sniff!
GNAP!

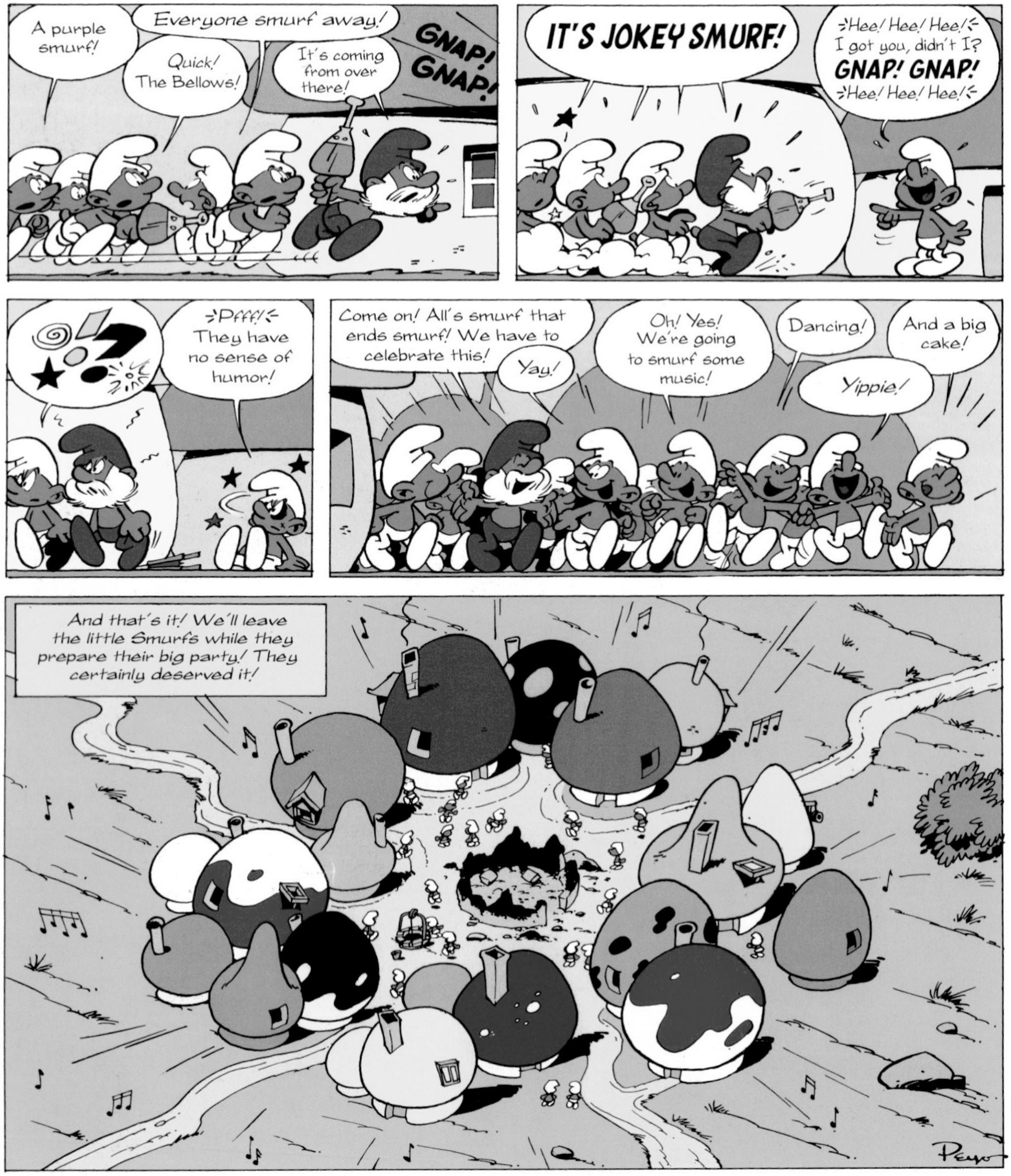

A purple smurf!
Everyone smurf away!
Quick! The Bellows!
It's coming from over there!
GNAP! GNAP!
IT'S JOKEY SMURF!
Hee! Hee! Hee! I got you, didn't I? GNAP! GNAP! Hee! Hee! Hee!
Pfff! They have no sense of humor!
Come on! All's smurf that ends smurf! We have to celebrate this!
Yay!
Oh! Yes! We're going to smurf some music!
Dancing!
Yippie!
And a big cake!
And that's it! We'll leave the little Smurfs while they prepare their big party! They certainly deserved it!
Peyo

END

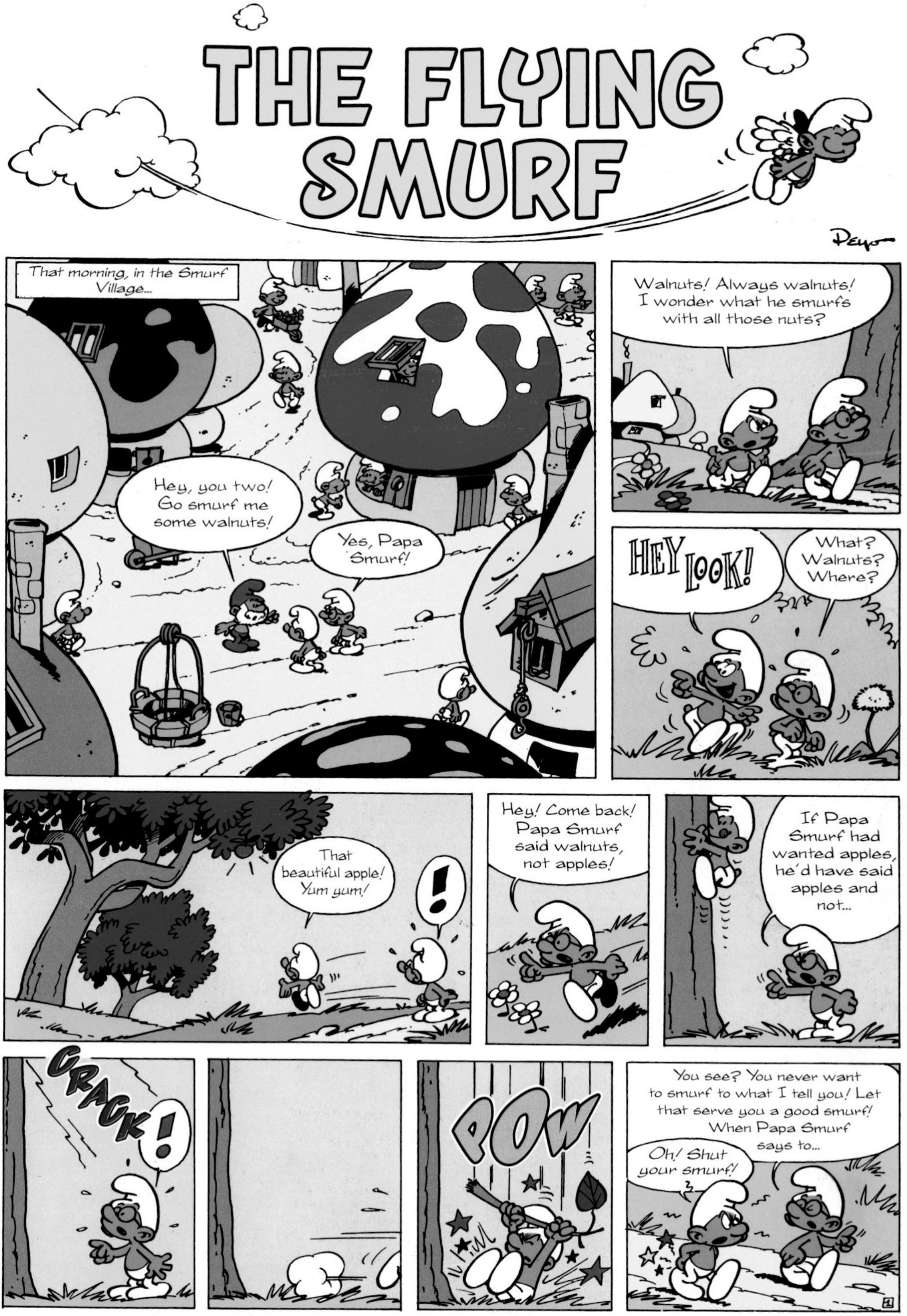
THE FLYING SMURF
Peyo
That morning, in the Smurf Village...
Hey, you two! Go smurf me some walnuts!
Yes, Papa Smurf!
Walnuts! Always walnuts! I wonder what he smurfs with all those nuts?
HEY LOOK!
What? Walnuts? Where?
That beautiful apple! Yum yum!
!
Hey! Come back! Papa Smurf said walnuts, not apples!
If Papa Smurf had wanted apples, he'd have said apples and not...
CRACK!
POW
You see? You never want to smurf to what I tell you! Let that serve you a good smurf! When Papa Smurf says to...
Oh! Shut your smurf!
1

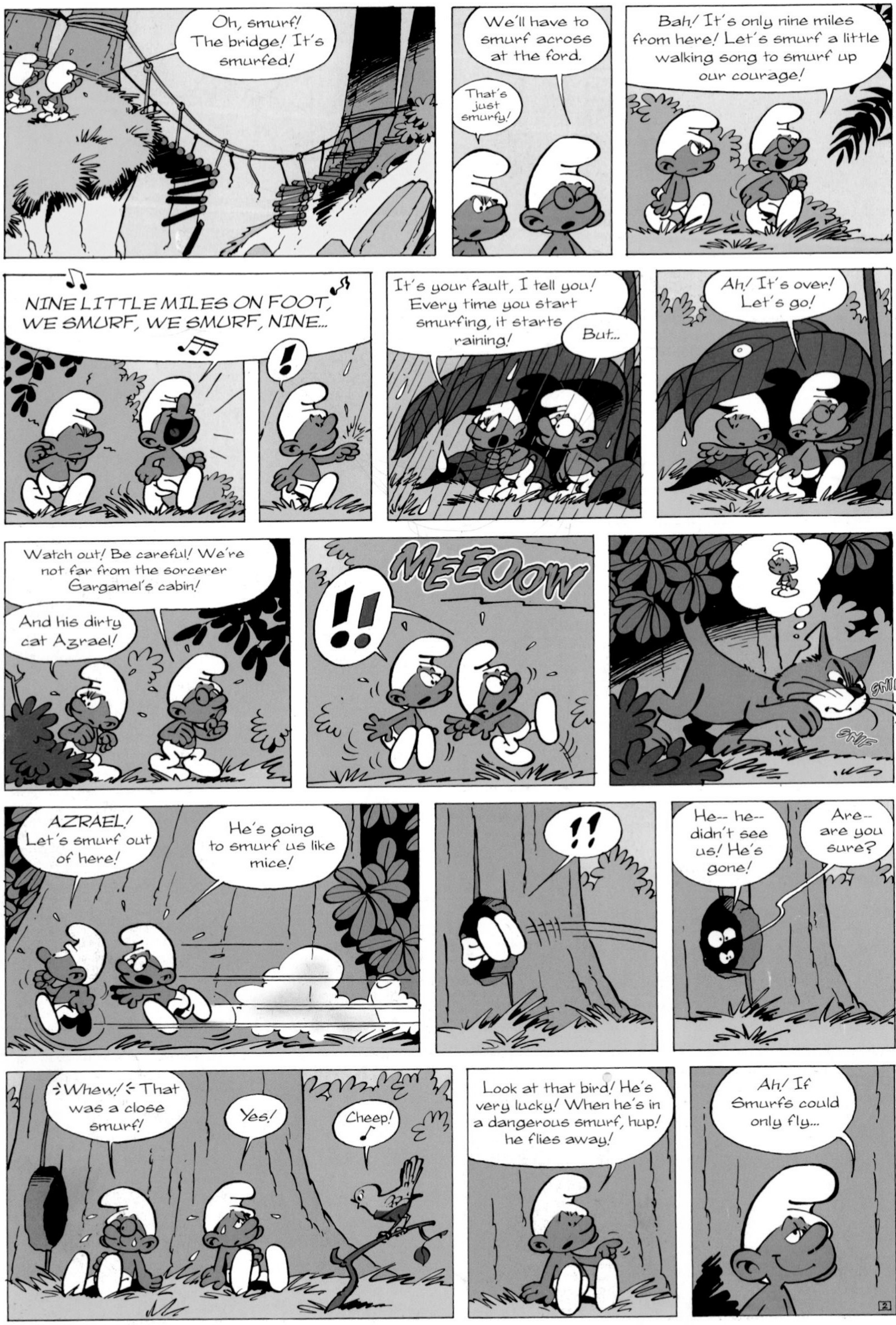

Oh, smurf! The bridge! It's smurfed!
We'll have to smurf across at the ford.
That's just smurfy!
Bah! It's only nine miles from here! Let's smurf a little walking song to smurf up our courage!
NINE LITTLE MILES ON FOOT, WE SMURF, WE SMURF, NINE...
!
It's your fault, I tell you! Every time you start smurfing, it starts raining!
But...
Ah! It's over! Let's go!
Watch out! Be careful! We're not far from the sorcerer Gargamel's cabin!
And his dirty cat Azrael!
MEEOOW
!!
SNIF
SNIF
AZRAEL! Let's smurf out of here!
He's going to smurf us like mice!
!!
He-- he-- didn't see us! He's gone!
Are-- are you sure?
Whew! That was a close smurf!
Yes!
Cheep!
Look at that bird! He's very lucky! When he's in a dangerous smurf, hup! he flies away!
Ah! If Smurfs could only fly...
2

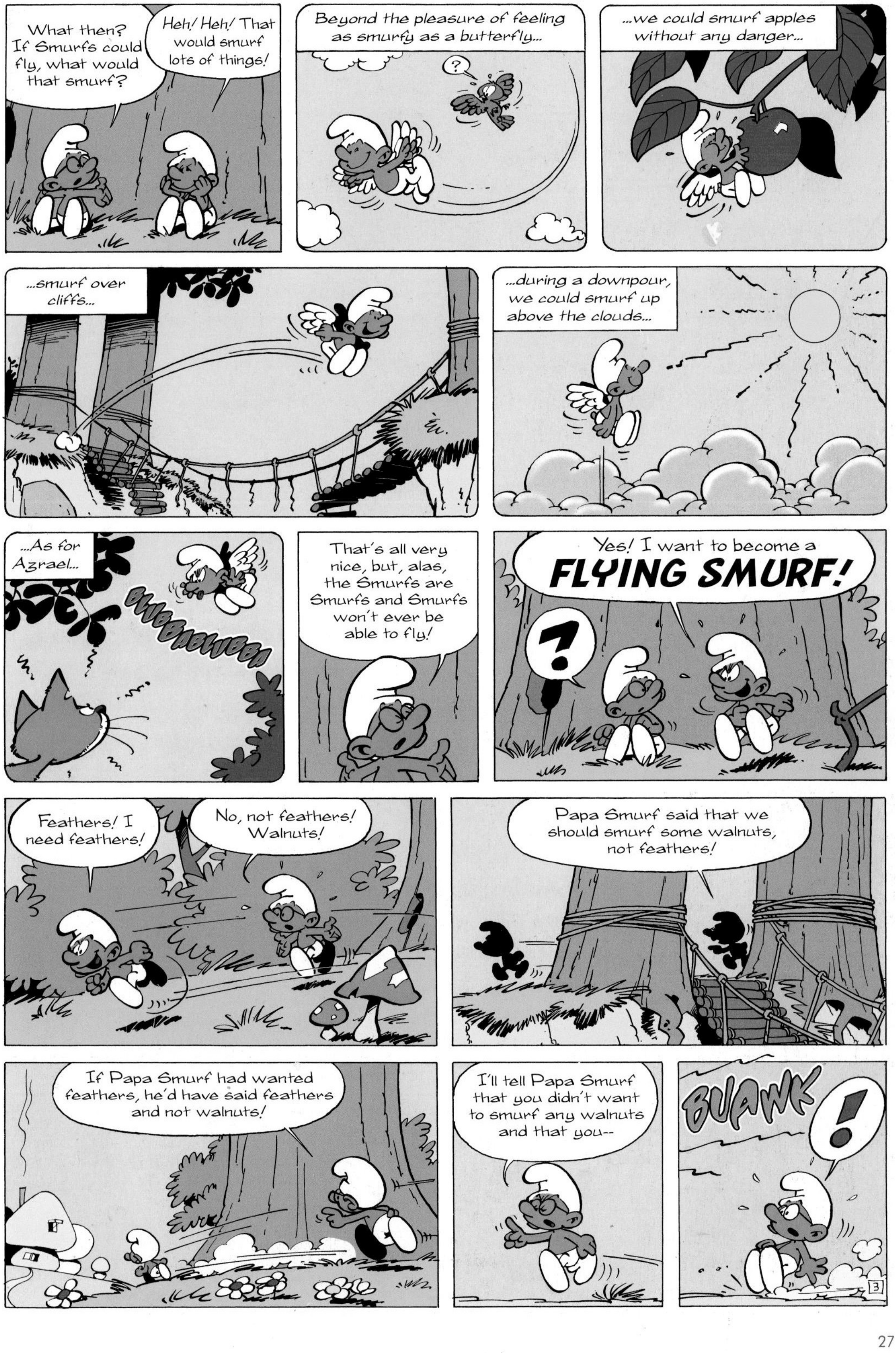

What then? If Smurfs could fly, what would that smurf?
Heh! Heh! That would smurf lots of things!
Beyond the pleasure of feeling as smurfy as a butterfly...
?
...we could smurf apples without any danger...
...smurf over cliffs...
...during a downpour, we could smurf up above the clouds...
...As for Azrael...
That's all very nice, but, alas, the Smurfs are Smurfs and Smurfs won't ever be able to fly!
Yes! I want to become a FLYING SMURF!
?
Feathers! I need feathers!
No, not feathers! Walnuts!
Papa Smurf said that we should smurf some walnuts, not feathers!
If Papa Smurf had wanted feathers, he'd have said feathers and not walnuts!
I'll tell Papa Smurf that you didn't want to smurf any walnuts and that you--
!

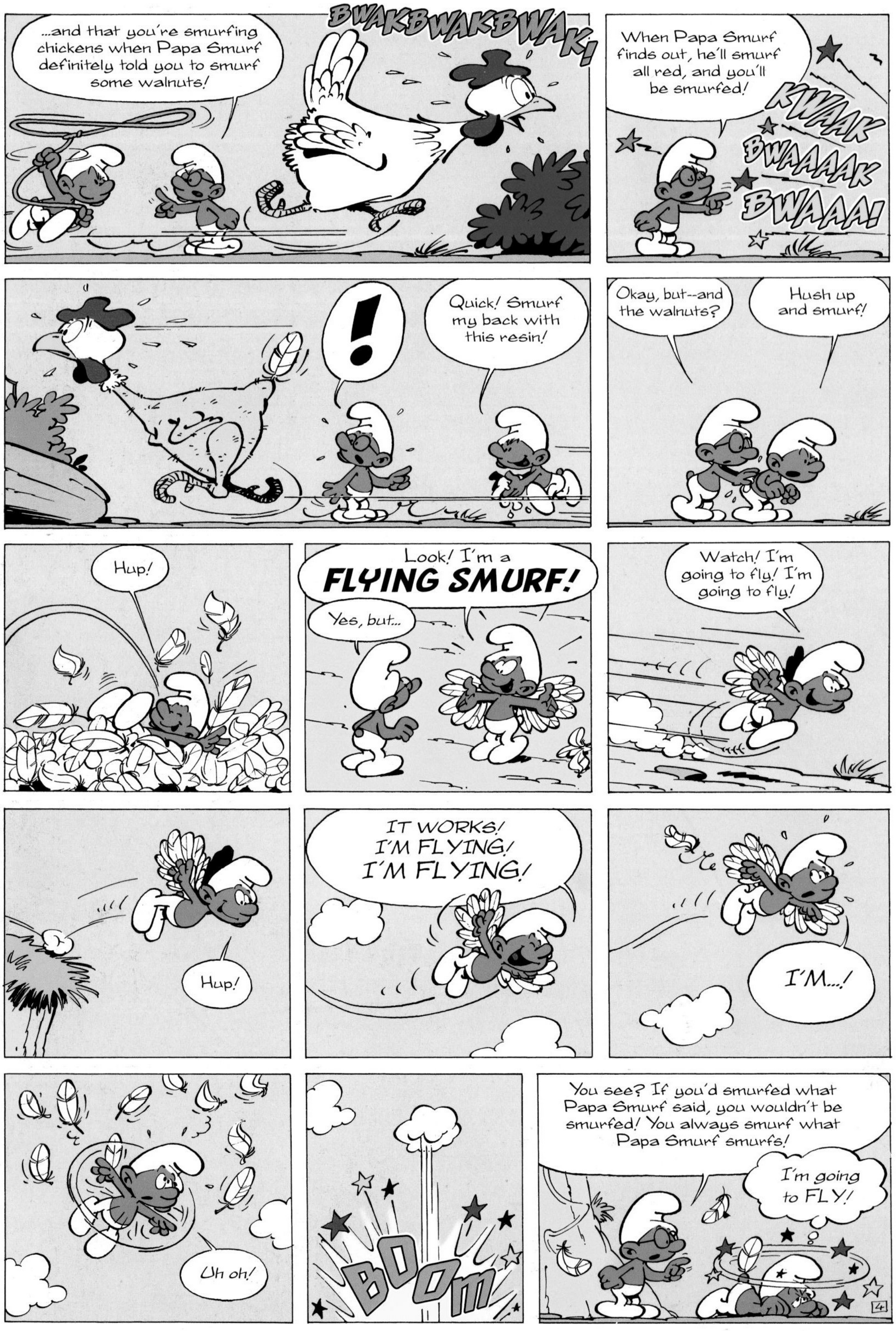
...and that you're smurfing chickens when Papa Smurf definitely told you to smurf some walnuts!
BWAKBWAKBWAK!
When Papa Smurf finds out, he'll smurf all red, and you'll be smurfed!
KWAAK
BWAAAAK
BWAAA!
!
Quick! Smurf my back with this resin!
Okay, but--and the walnuts?
Hush up and smurf!
Hup!
Look! I'm a FLYING SMURF!
Yes, but...
Watch! I'm going to fly! I'm going to fly!
Hup!
IT WORKS! I'M FLYING! I'M FLYING!
I'M...!
Uh oh!
BOOM
You see? If you'd smurfed what Papa Smurf said, you wouldn't be smurfed! You always smurf what Papa Smurf smurfs!
I'm going to FLY!
4

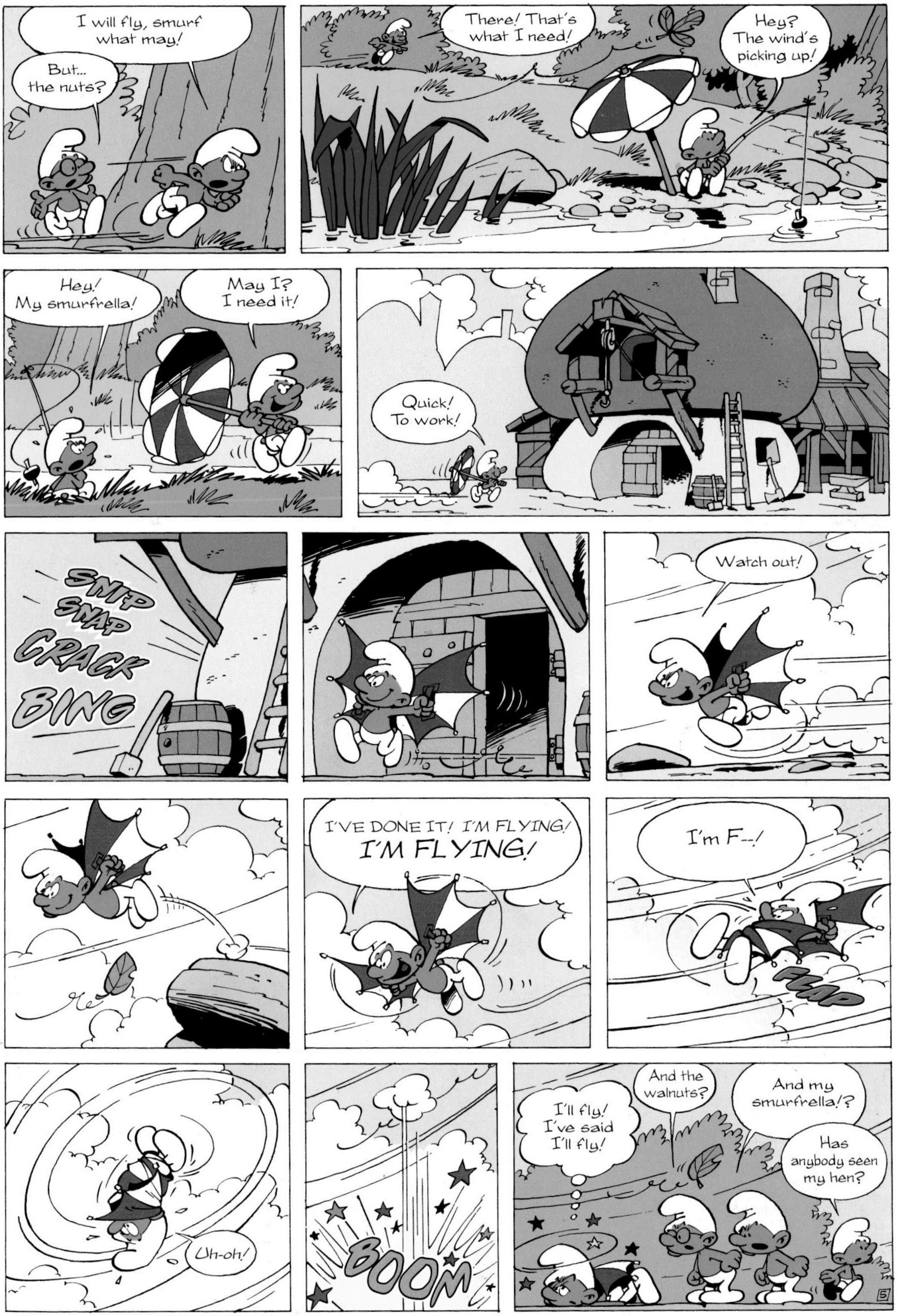
I will fly, smurf what may!
But... the nuts?
There! That's what I need!
Hey? The wind's picking up!
Hey! My smurfrella!
May I? I need it!
Quick! To work!
SNIP
SNAP
CRACK
BING
Watch out!
I'VE DONE IT! I'M FLYING! I'M FLYING!
I'm F--!
FLAP
Uh-oh!
BOOM
I'll fly! I've said I'll fly!
And the walnuts?
And my smurfrella!?
Has anybody seen my hen?
5

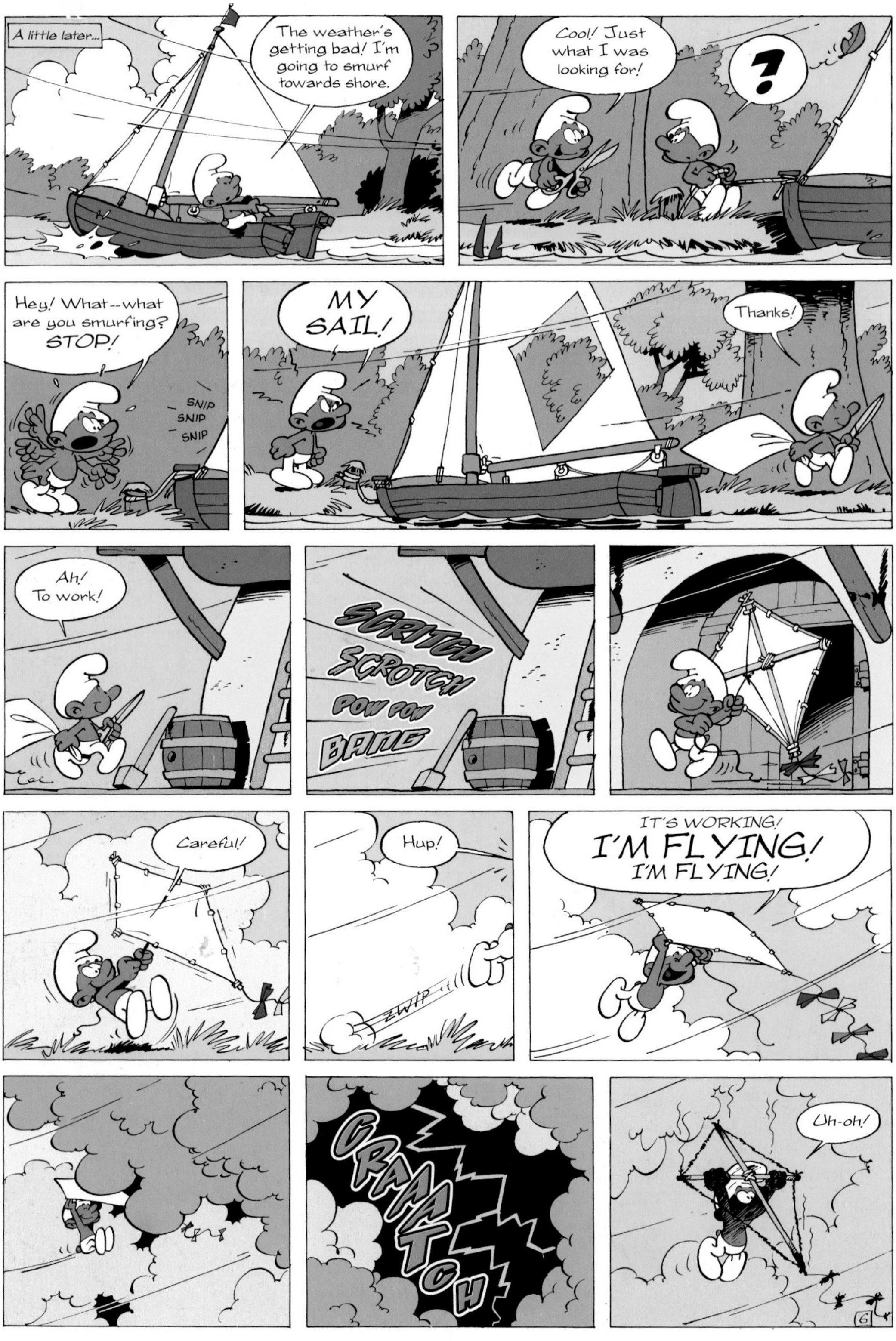
A little later...
The weather's getting bad! I'm going to smurf towards shore.
Cool! Just what I was looking for!
?
Hey! What--what are you smurfing? STOP!
SNIP
SNIP
SNIP
MY SAIL!
Thanks!
Ah! To work!
SCRITCH
SCROTCH
POW POW
BANG
Careful!
Hup!
ZWIP
IT'S WORKING!
I'M FLYING!
I'M FLYING!
CRAAATCH
Uh-oh!
6

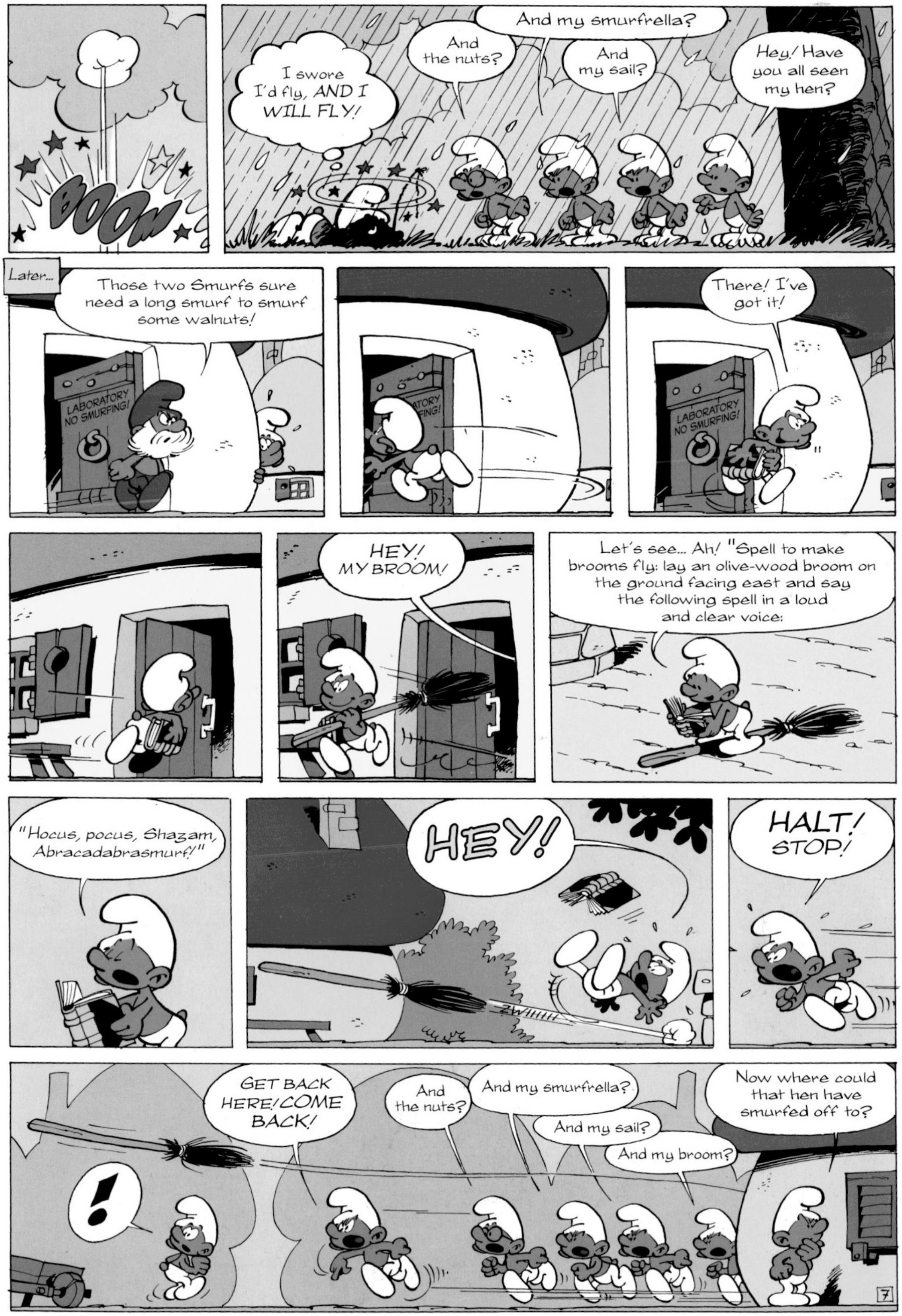
BOOOM
I swore I'd fly, AND I WILL FLY!
And the nuts?
And my smurfrella?
And my sail?
Hey! Have you all seen my hen?
Later...
Those two Smurfs sure need a long smurf to smurf some walnuts!
LABORATORY NO SMURFING!
There! I've got it!
HEY! MY BROOM!
Let's see... Ah! "Spell to make brooms fly: lay an olive-wood broom on the ground facing east and say the following spell in a loud and clear voice:
"Hocus, pocus, Shazam, Abracadabrasmurf!"
HEY!
HALT! STOP!
!
GET BACK HERE! COME BACK!
And the nuts?
And my smurfrella?
And my sail?
And my broom?
Now where could that hen have smurfed off to?
7

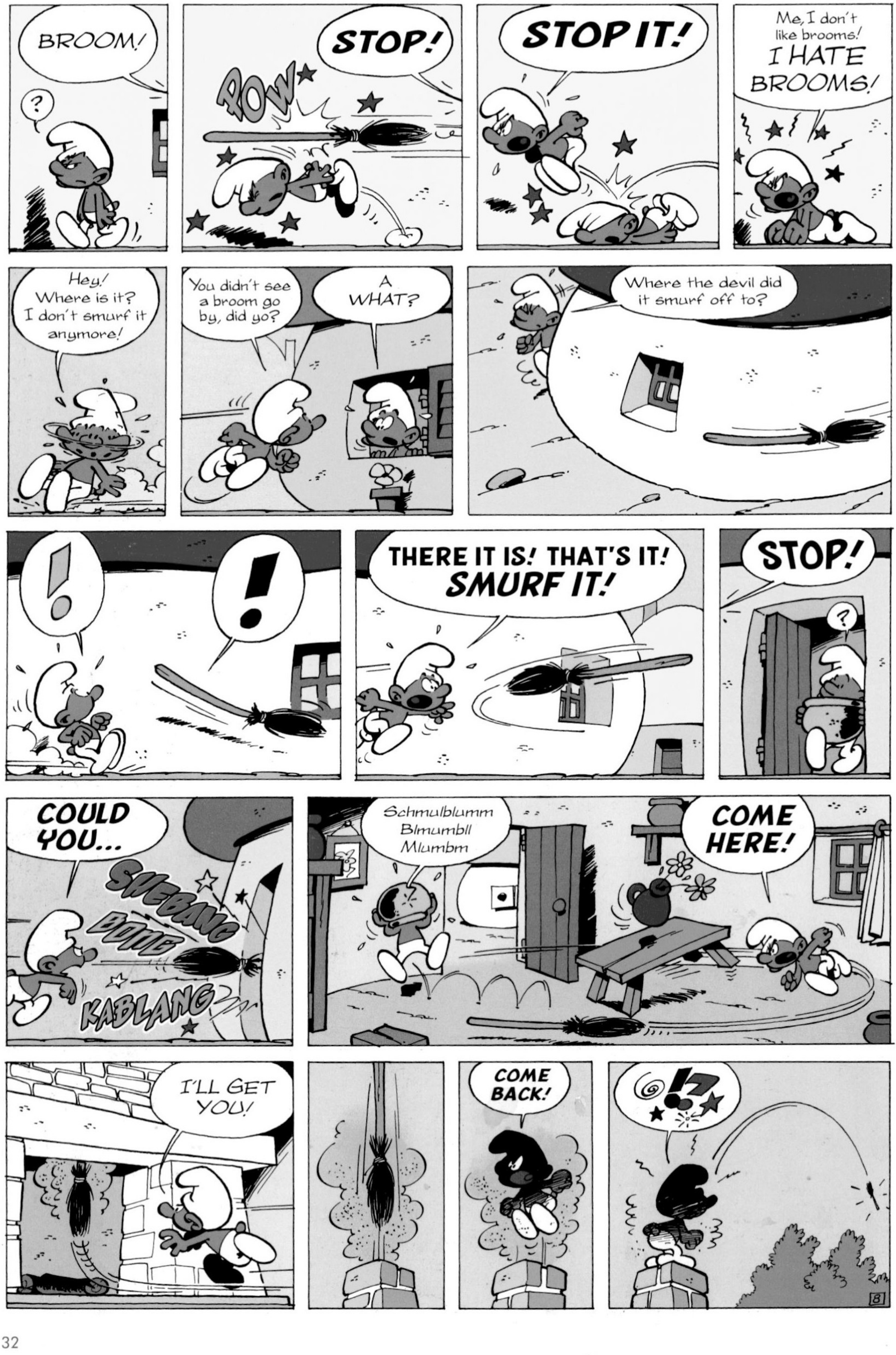
BROOM!
?
POW
STOP!
STOP IT!
Me, I don't like brooms! I HATE BROOMS!
Hey! Where is it? I don't smurf it anymore!
You didn't see a broom go by, did yo?
A WHAT?
Where the devil did it smurf off to?
!
!
THERE IT IS! THAT'S IT! SMURF IT!
STOP!
?
COULD YOU...
SHEBANG
BONG
KABLANG
Schmulblumm Blmumbll Mlumbm
COME HERE!
I'LL GET YOU!
COME BACK!
8

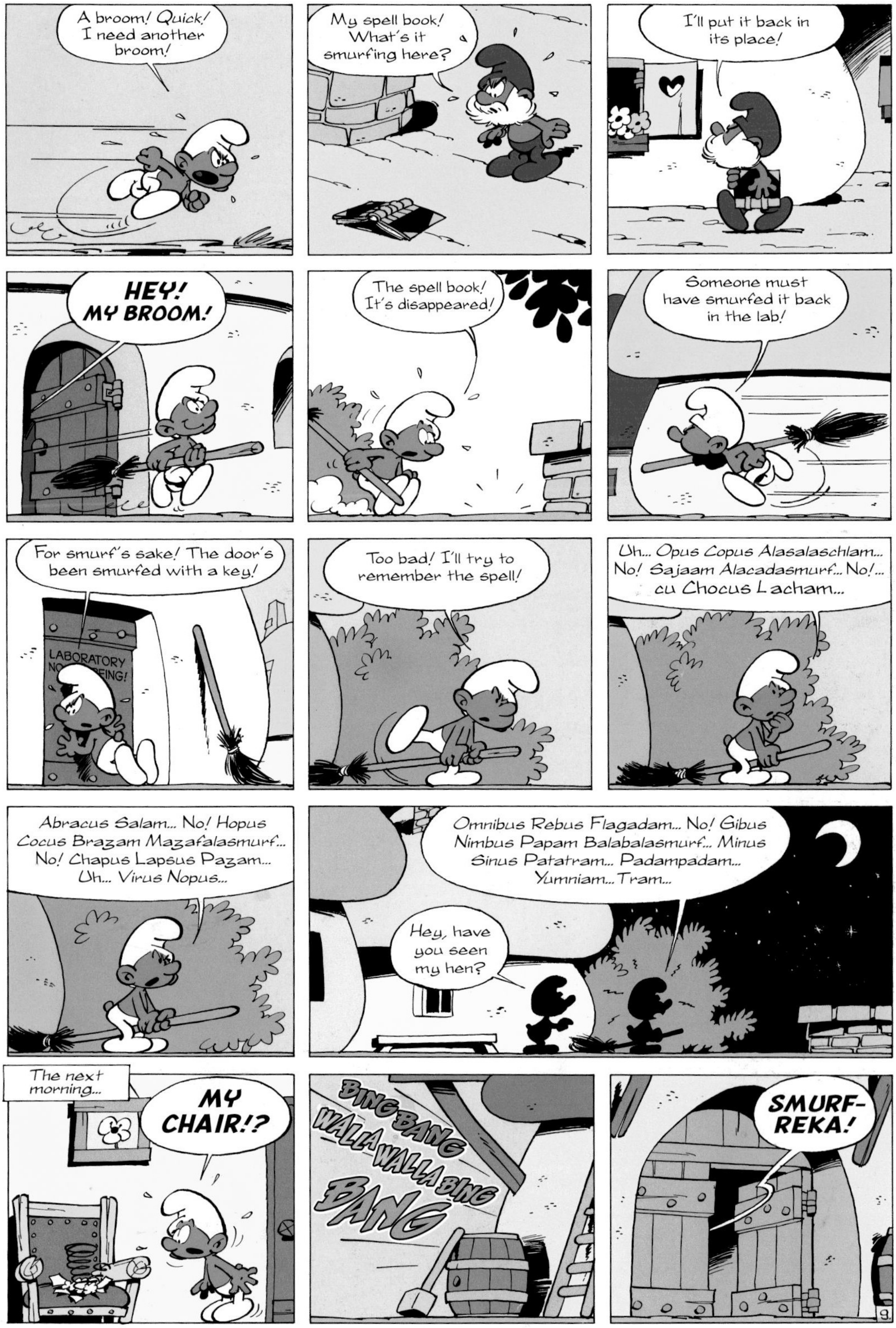
A broom! Quick! I need another broom!
My spell book! What's it smurfing here?
I'll put it back in its place!
HEY! MY BROOM!
The spell book! It's disappeared!
Someone must have smurfed it back in the lab!
For smurf's sake! The door's been smurfed with a key!
LABORATORY NO ...ING!
Too bad! I'll try to remember the spell!
Uh... Opus Copus Alasalaschlam... No! Sajaam Alacadasmurf... No!... cu Chocus Lacham...
Abracus Salam... No! Hopus Cocus Brazam Mazafalasmurf... No! Chapus Lapsus Pazam... Uh... Virus Nopus...
Omnibus Rebus Flagadam... No! Gibus Nimbus Papam Balabalasmurf... Minus Sinus Patatram... Padampadam... Yumniam... Tram...
Hey, have you seen my hen?
The next morning...
MY CHAIR!?
BING BANG WALLA WALLA BING BANG
SMURF-REKA!
9

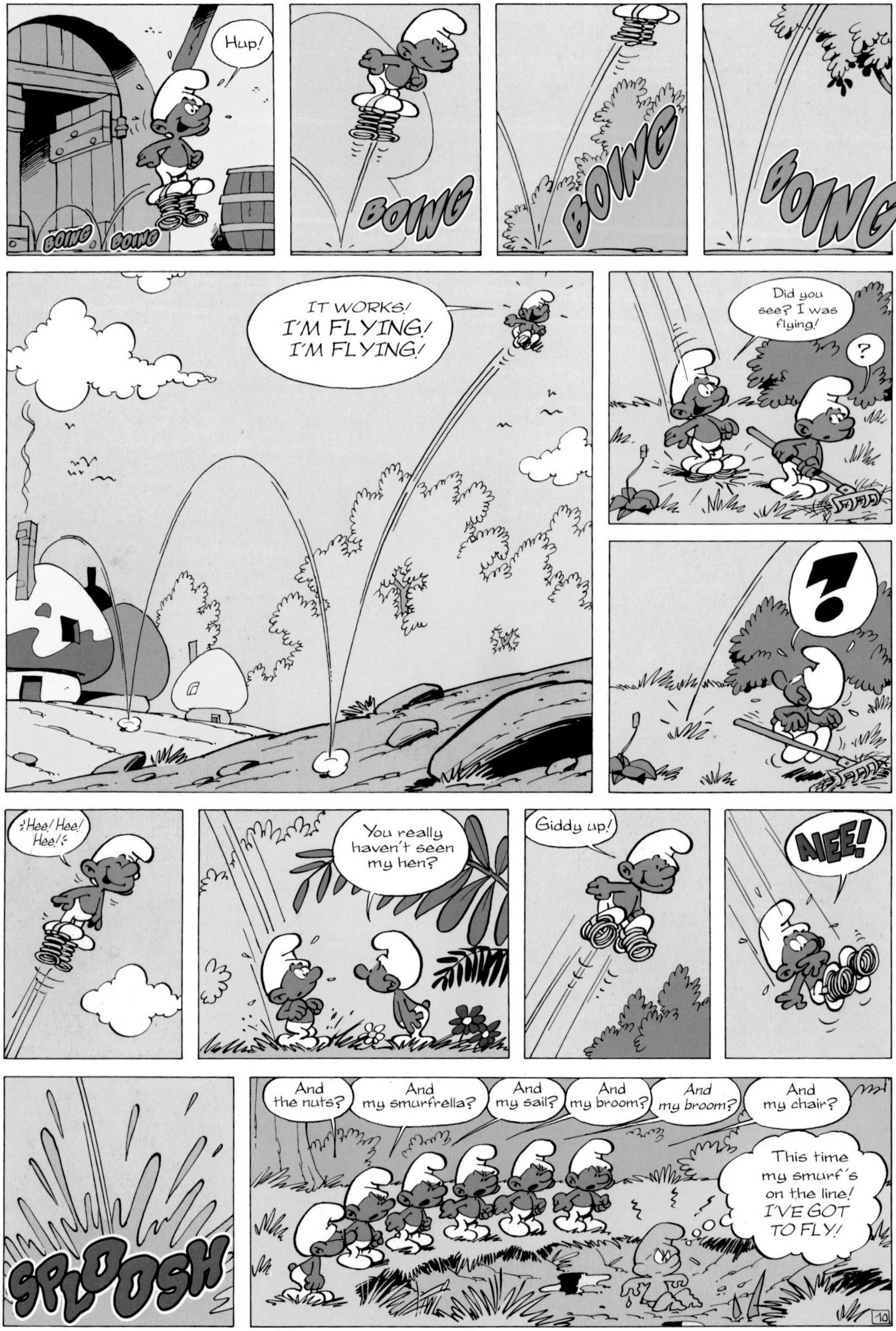
Hup!
BOING BOING
BOING
BOING
BOING
IT WORKS! I'M FLYING! I'M FLYING!
Did you see? I was flying!
?
?
Hee! Hee! Hee!
You really haven't seen my hen?
Giddy up!
AIEE!
SPLOOSH
And the nuts?
And my smurfrella?
And my sail?
And my broom?
And my broom?
And my chair?
This time my smurf's on the line! I'VE GOT TO FLY!
10

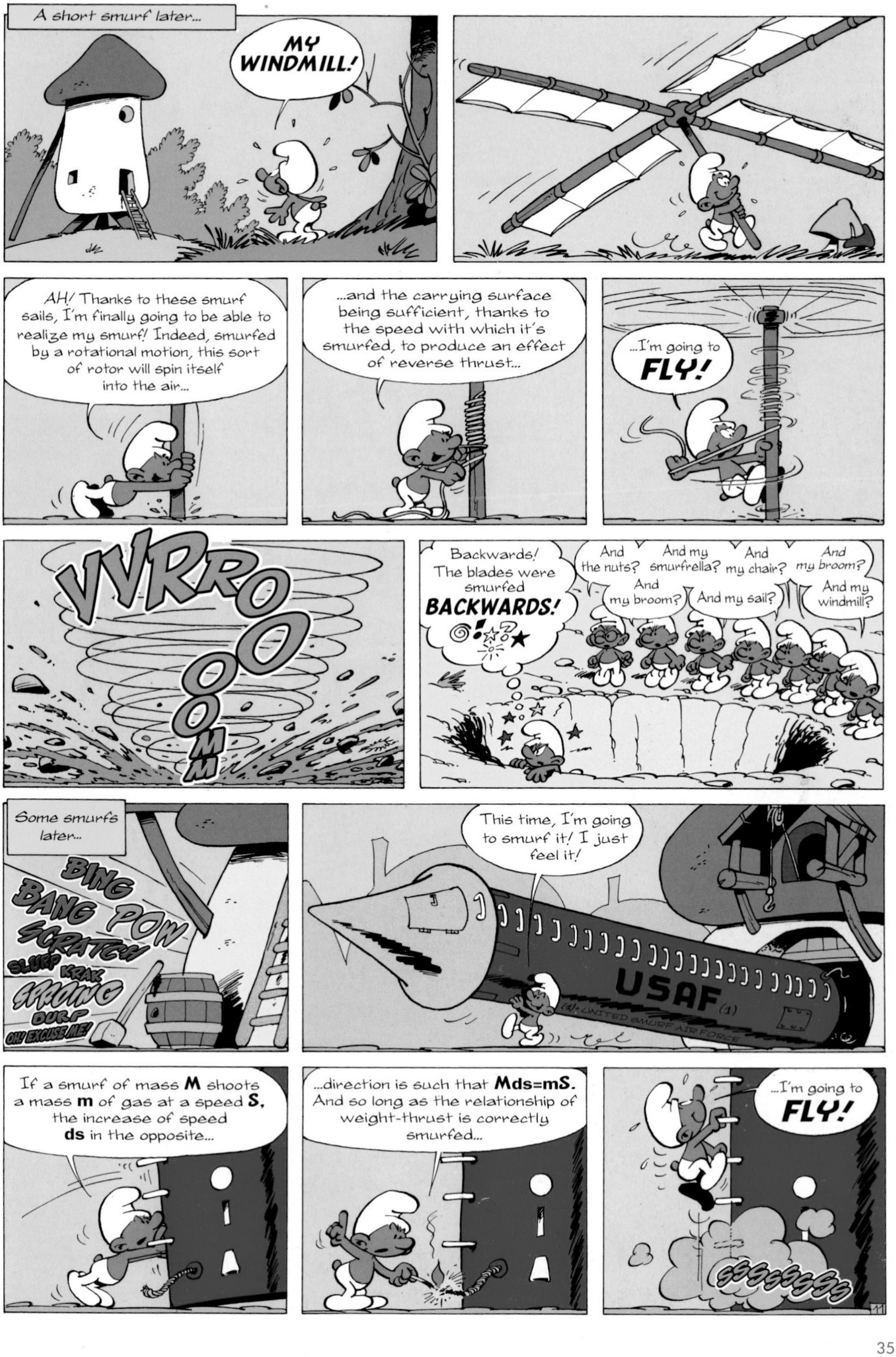
A short smurf later...
MY WINDMILL!
AH! Thanks to these smurf sails, I'm finally going to be able to realize my smurf! Indeed, smurfed by a rotational motion, this sort of rotor will spin itself into the air...
...and the carrying surface being sufficient, thanks to the speed with which it's smurfed, to produce an effect of reverse thrust...
...I'm going to FLY!
VVRROOOOOMM
Backwards! The blades were smurfed BACKWARDS!
And the nuts?
And my smurfrella?
And my chair?
And my broom?
And my broom?
And my sail?
And my windmill?
Some smurfs later...
BING
BANG POW
SCRATCH
SLURP KRAK
SPROING
BURP
OH! EXCUSE ME!
This time, I'm going to smurf it! I just feel it!
USAF(1)
(1): UNITED SMURF AIR FORCE
If a smurf of mass M shoots a mass m of gas at a speed S, the increase of speed ds in the opposite...
...direction is such that Mds=mS. And so long as the relationship of weight-thrust is correctly smurfed...
...I'm going to FLY!
SSSSSSSSS
11

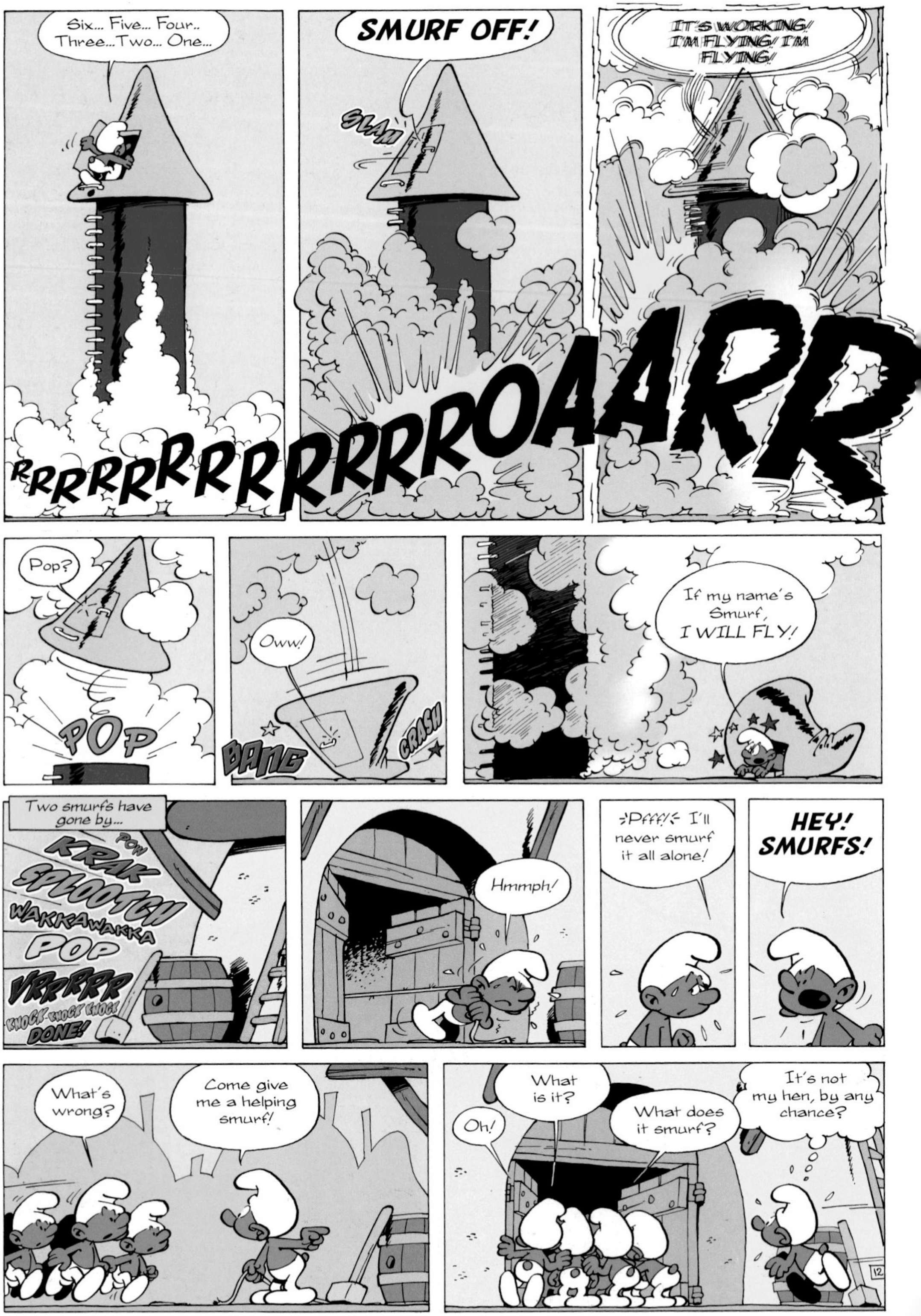
Six... Five... Four..
Three...Two... One...
SMURF OFF!
SLAM
IT'S WORKING! I'M FLYING! I'M FLYING!
RRRRRRRRRRRRROAARR
Pop?
POP
Oww!
BANG
CRASH
If my name's Smurf, I WILL FLY!
Two smurfs have gone by...
POW
KRAK
SPLOOTCH
WAKKAWAKKA
POP
VRRRRR
KNOCK KNOCK KNOCK
DONE!
Hmmph!
Pfff! I'll never smurf it all alone!
HEY! SMURFS!
What's wrong?
Come give me a helping smurf!
Oh!
What is it?
What does it smurf?
It's not my hen, by any chance?
12

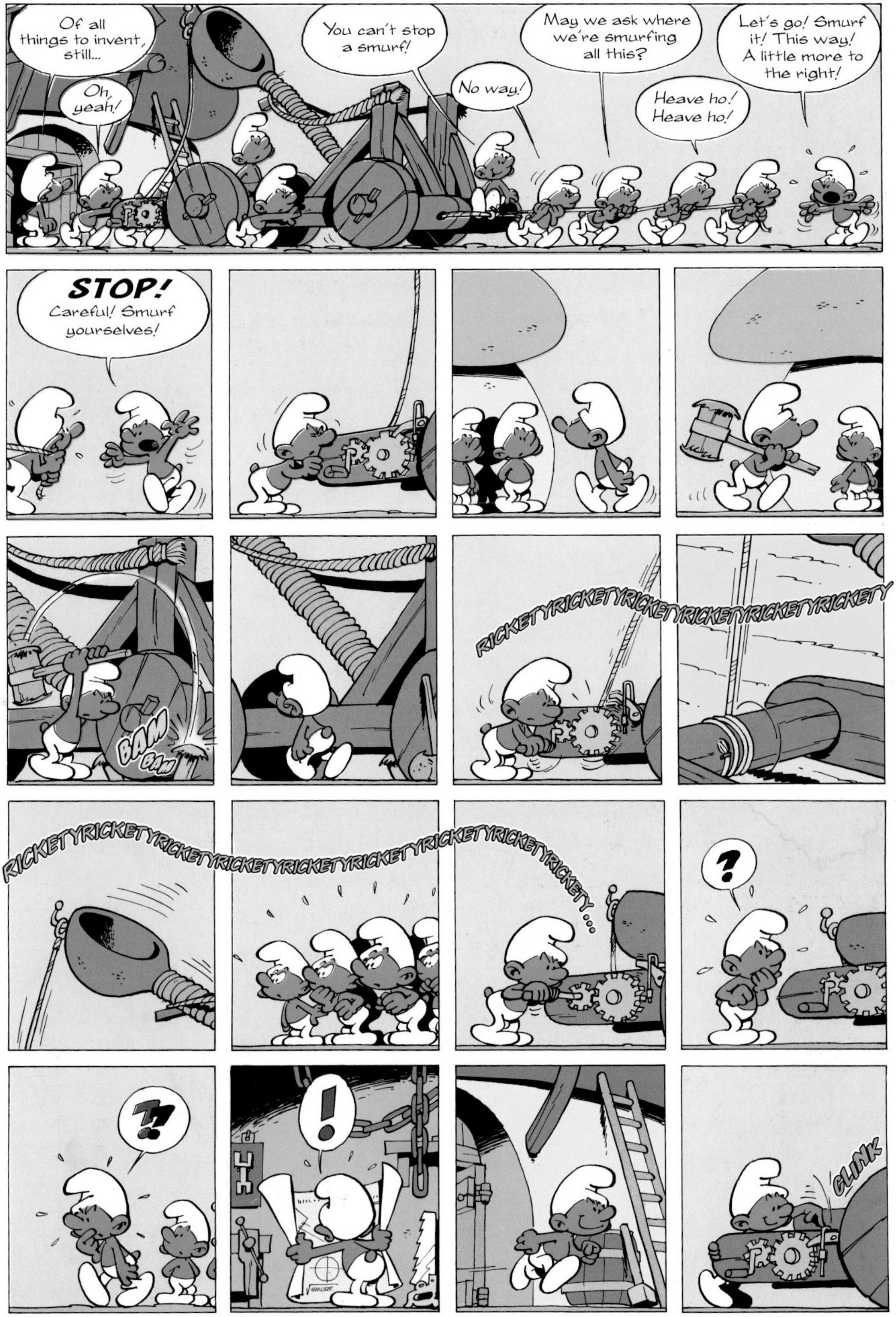
Of all things to invent, still...
Oh, yeah!
You can't stop a smurf!
No way!
May we ask where we're smurfing all this?
Heave ho! Heave ho!
Let's go! Smurf it! This way! A little more to the right!
STOP! Careful! Smurf yourselves!
BAM BAM
RICKETYRICKETYRICKETYRICKETYRICKETYRICKETY
RICKETYRICKETYRICKETYRICKETYRICKETYRICKETYRICKETYRICKETYRICKETY...
?
?!
!
CLINK

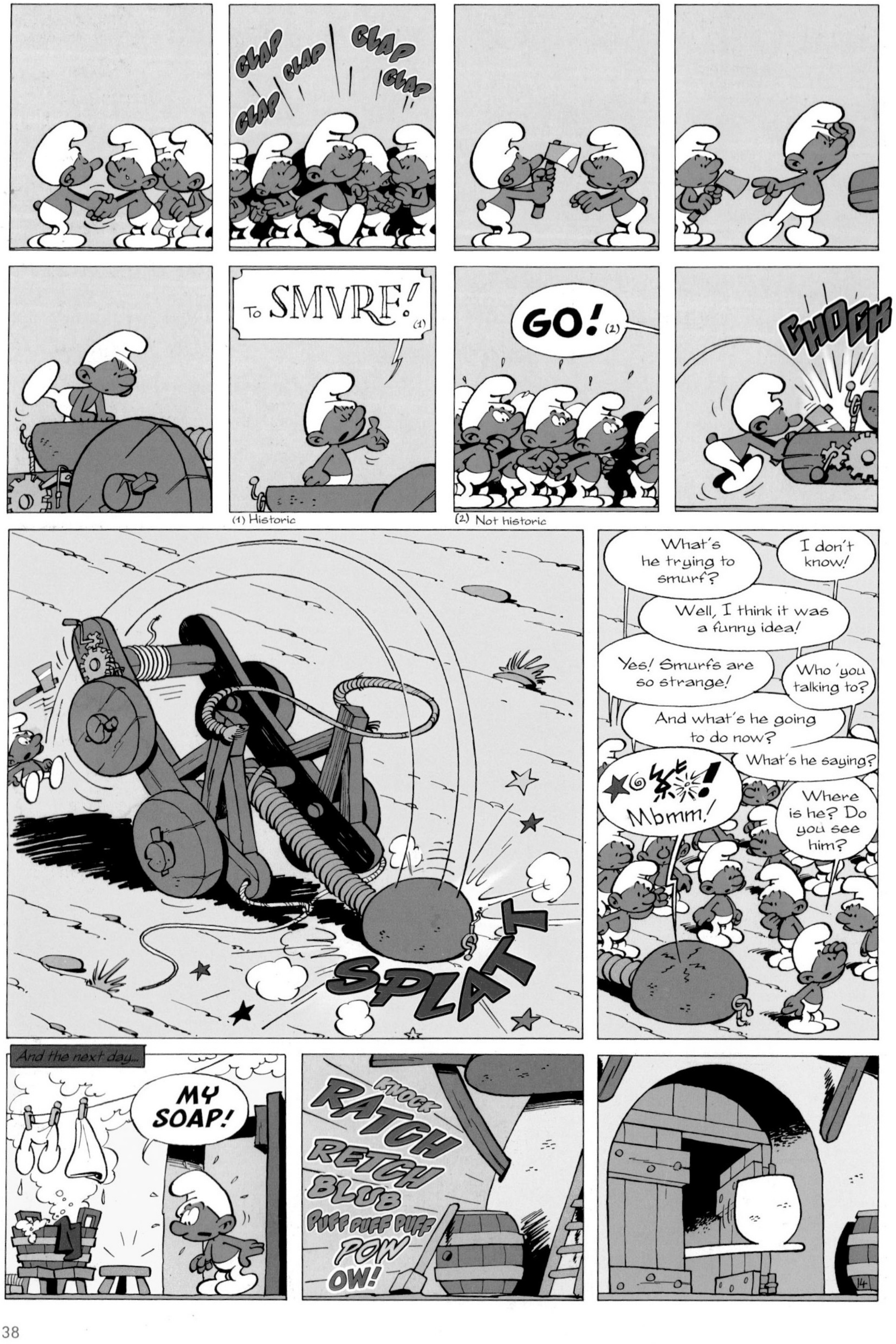
CLAP
CLAP
CLAP
CLAP
CLAP
To SMVRF! (1)
GO! (2)
CHOCK
SPLATT
What's he trying to smurf?
I don't know!
Well, I think it was a funny idea!
Yes! Smurfs are so strange!
Who 'you talking to?
And what's he going to do now?
What's he saying?
Mbmm!
Where is he? Do you see him?
And the next day...
MY SOAP!
KNOCK
RATCH
RETCH
BLUB
PUFF PUFF PUFF
POW
OW!

(1) Historic

(2) Not historic

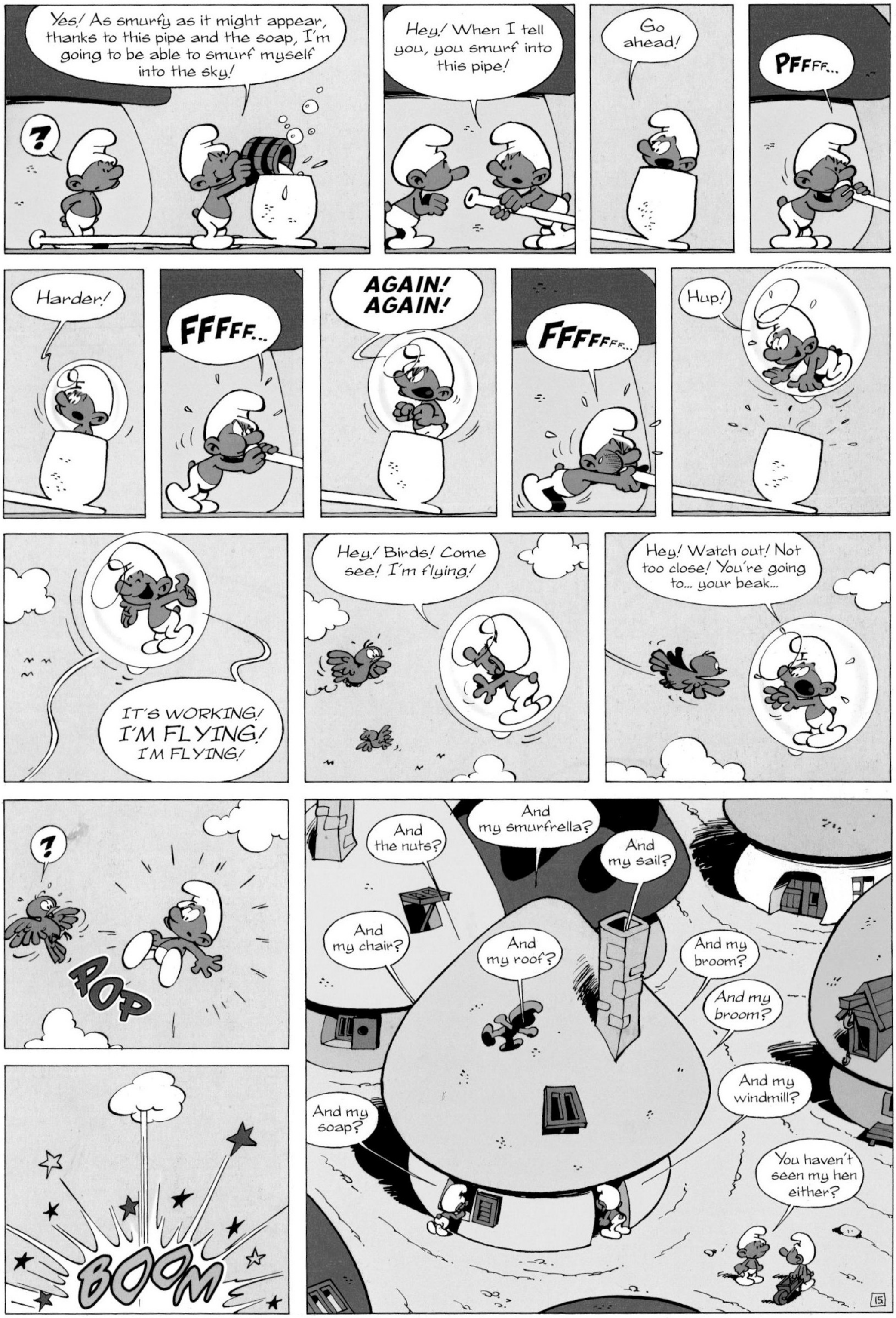
Yes! As smurfy as it might appear, thanks to this pipe and the soap, I'm going to be able to smurf myself into the sky!
?
Hey! When I tell you, you smurf into this pipe!
Go ahead!
PFFFF...
Harder!
FFFFF...
AGAIN! AGAIN!
FFFFFFF...
Hup!
IT'S WORKING! I'M FLYING! I'M FLYING!
Hey! Birds! Come see! I'm flying!
Hey! Watch out! Not too close! You're going to... your beak...
?
POP
BOOM
And the nuts?
And my smurfrella?
And my sail?
And my chair?
And my roof?
And my broom?
And my broom?
And my windmill?
And my soap?
You haven't seen my hen either?
15

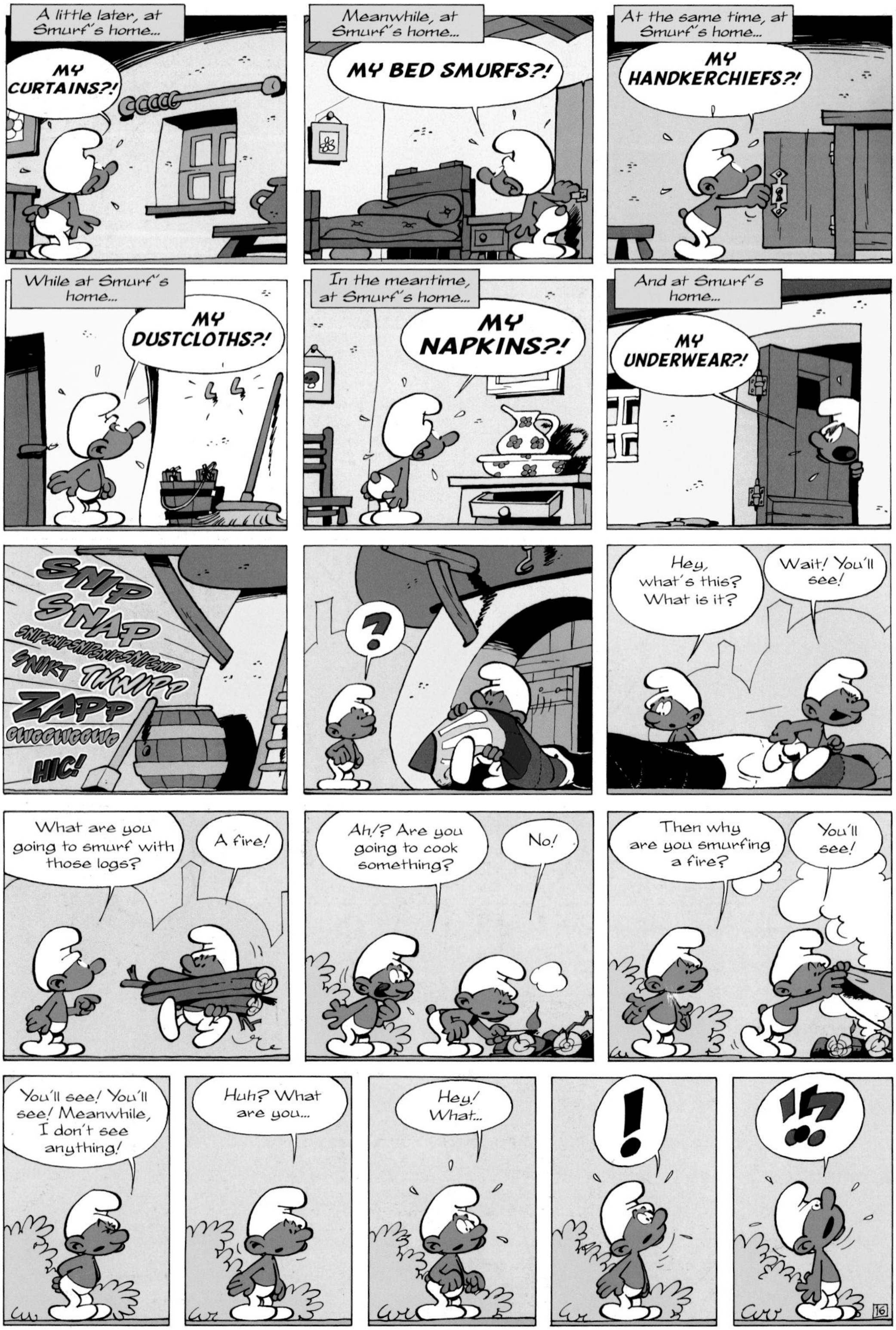

A little later, at Smurf's home...
MY CURTAINS?!
Meanwhile, at Smurf's home...
MY BED SMURFS?!
At the same time, at Smurf's home...
MY HANDKERCHIEFS?!
While at Smurf's home...
MY DUSTCLOTHS?!
In the meantime, at Smurf's home...
MY NAPKINS?!
And at Smurf's home...
MY UNDERWEAR?!
SNIP
SNAP
SNIKT
THWIPP
ZAPP
HIC!
?
Hey, what's this? What is it?
Wait! You'll see!
What are you going to smurf with those logs?
A fire!
Ah!? Are you going to cook something?
No!
Then why are you smurfing a fire?
You'll see!
You'll see! You'll see! Meanwhile, I don't see anything!
Huh? What are you...
Hey! What...
!
!?

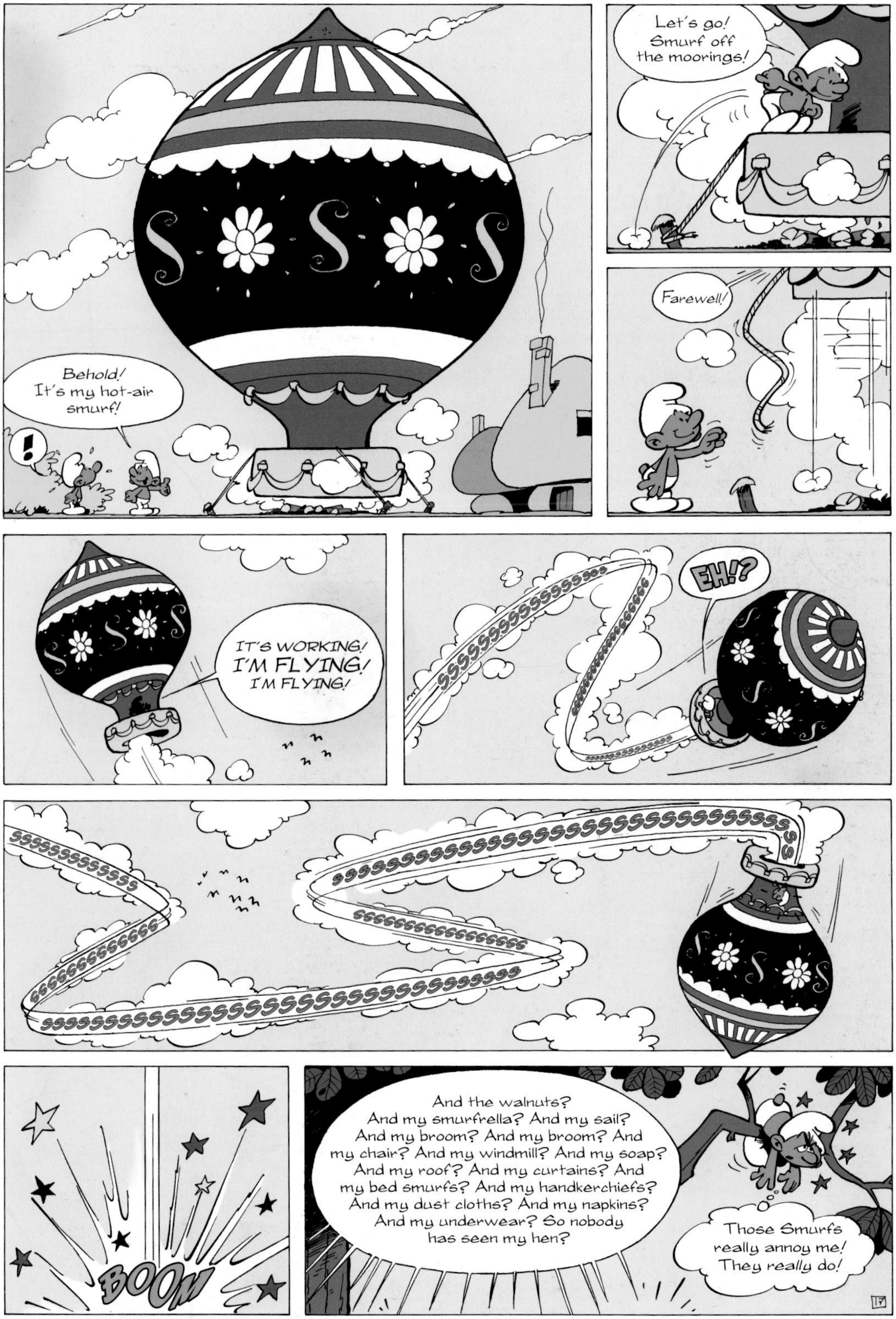
Behold! It's my hot-air smurf!
!
Let's go! Smurf off the moorings!
Farewell!
IT'S WORKING! I'M FLYING! I'M FLYING!
EH!?
BOOM
And the walnuts? And my smurfrella? And my sail? And my broom? And my broom? And my chair? And my windmill? And my soap? And my roof? And my curtains? And my bed smurfs? And my handkerchiefs? And my dust cloths? And my napkins? And my underwear? So nobody has seen my hen?
Those Smurfs really annoy me! They really do!
17

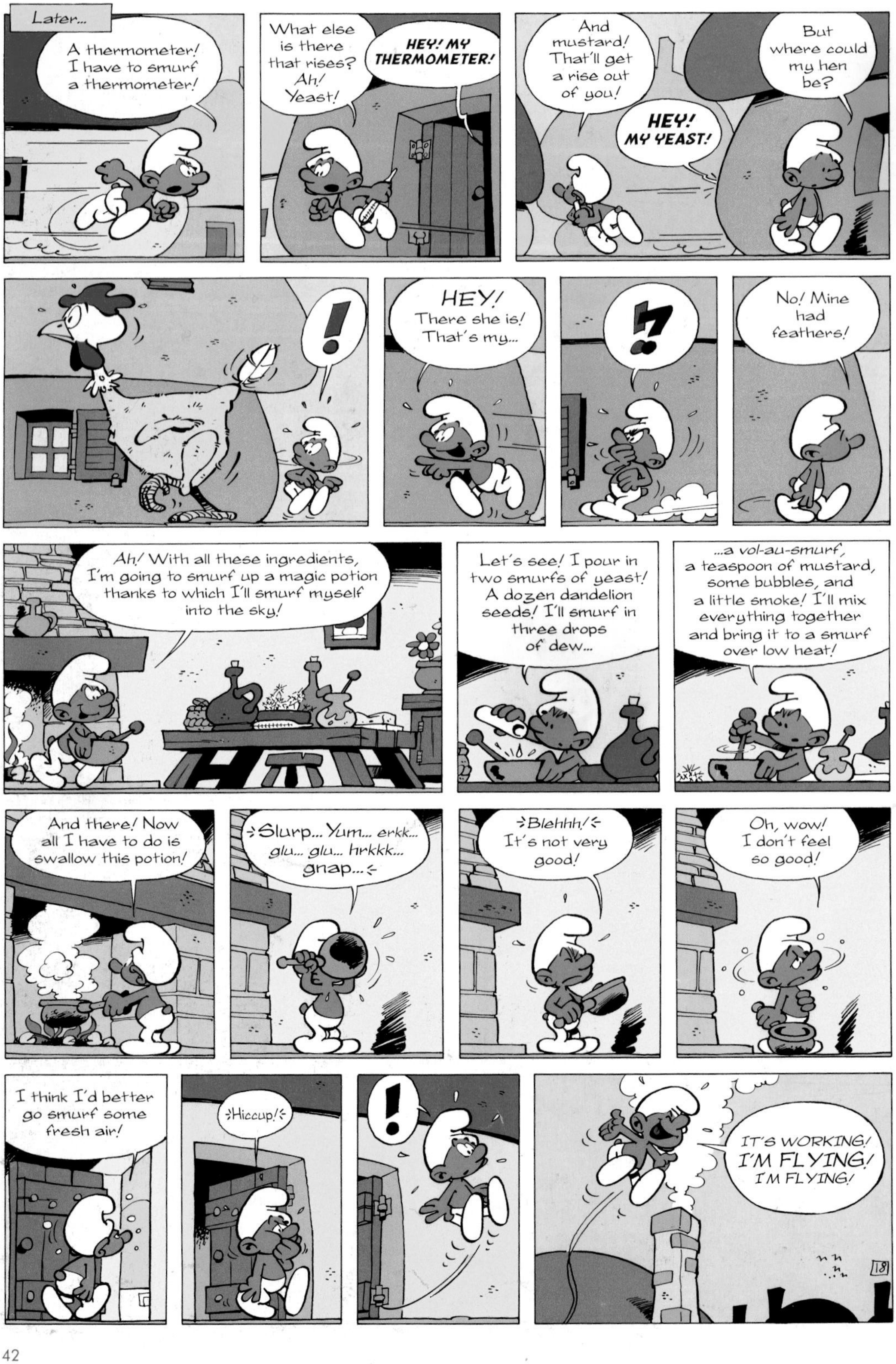
Later...
A thermometer! I have to smurf a thermometer!
What else is there that rises? Ah! Yeast!
HEY! MY THERMOMETER!
And mustard! That'll get a rise out of you!
HEY! MY YEAST!
But where could my hen be?
!
HEY! There she is! That's my...
?
No! Mine had feathers!
Ah! With all these ingredients, I'm going to smurf up a magic potion thanks to which I'll smurf myself into the sky!
Let's see! I pour in two smurfs of yeast! A dozen dandelion seeds! I'll smurf in three drops of dew...
...a vol-au-smurf, a teaspoon of mustard, some bubbles, and a little smoke! I'll mix everything together and bring it to a smurf over low heat!
And there! Now all I have to do is swallow this potion!
Slurp... Yum... erkk... glu... glu... hrkkk... gnap...
Blehhh! It's not very good!
Oh, wow! I don't feel so good!
I think I'd better go smurf some fresh air!
Hiccup!
!
IT'S WORKING! I'M FLYING! I'M FLYING!
18

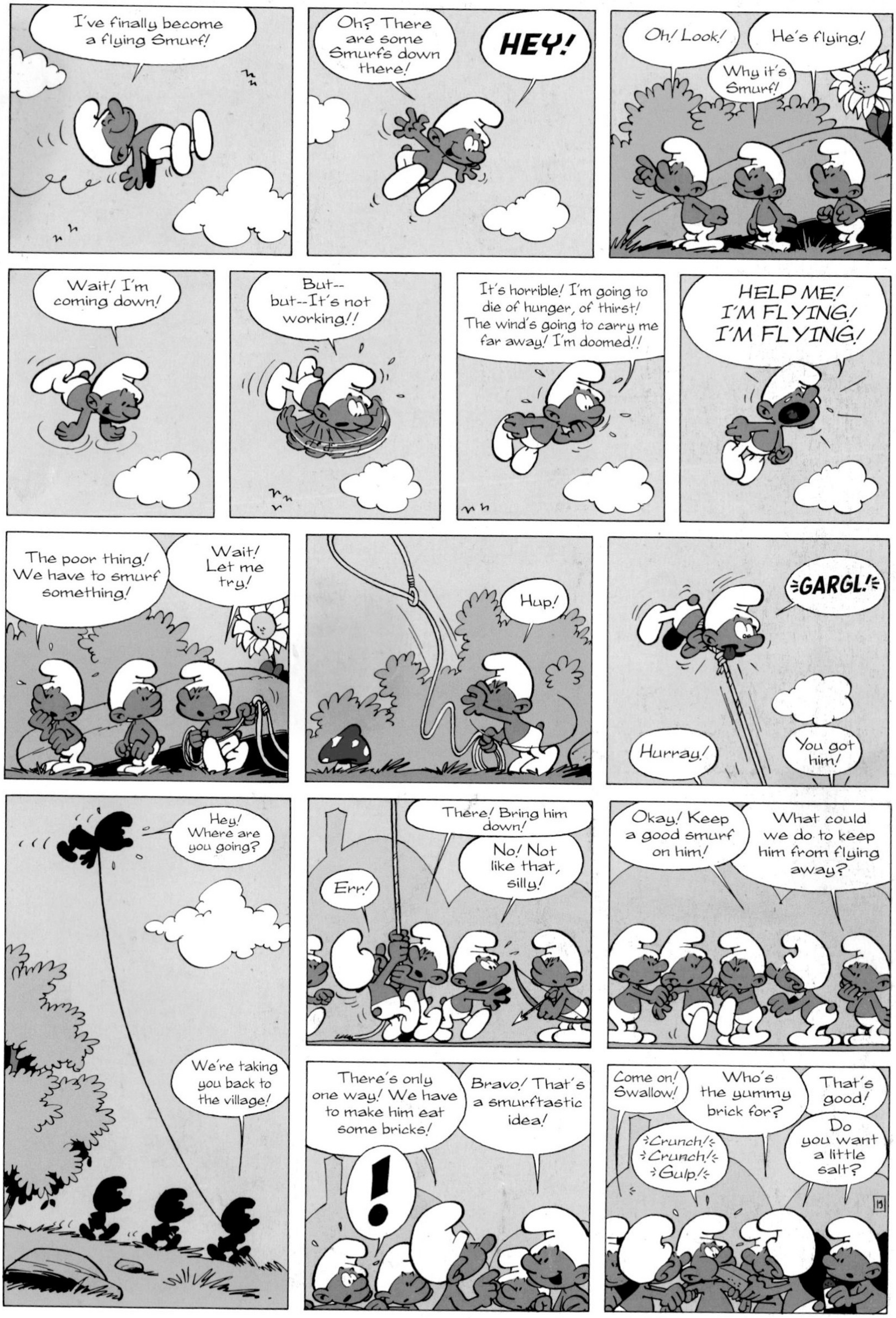
I've finally become a flying Smurf!
Oh? There are some Smurfs down there!
HEY!
Oh! Look!
Why it's Smurf!
He's flying!
Wait! I'm coming down!
But-- but--It's not working!!
It's horrible! I'm going to die of hunger, of thirst! The wind's going to carry me far away! I'm doomed!!
HELP ME! I'M FLYING! I'M FLYING!
The poor thing! We have to smurf something!
Wait! Let me try!
Hup!
GARGL!
Hurray!
You got him!
Hey! Where are you going?
We're taking you back to the village!
There! Bring him down!
Err!
No! Not like that, silly!
Okay! Keep a good smurf on him!
What could we do to keep him from flying away?
There's only one way! We have to make him eat some bricks!
Bravo! That's a smurftastic idea!
!
Come on! Swallow!
Who's the yummy brick for?
Crunch! Crunch! Gulp!
That's good!
Do you want a little salt?
15

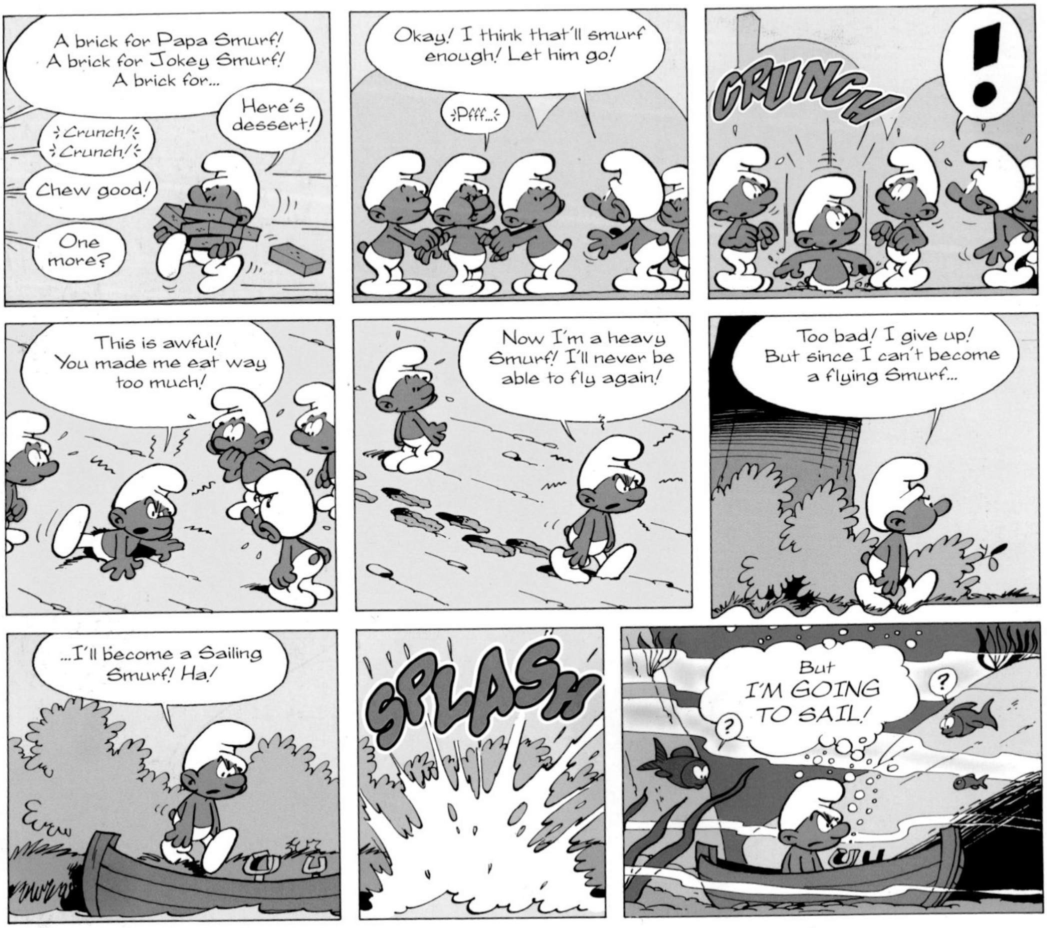
A brick for Papa Smurf! A brick for Jokey Smurf! A brick for...
Crunch! Crunch!
Here's dessert!
Chew good!
One more?
Okay! I think that'll smurf enough! Let him go!
Pfff...
CRUNCH
!
This is awful! You made me eat way too much!
Now I'm a heavy Smurf! I'll never be able to fly again!
Too bad! I give up! But since I can't become a flying Smurf...
...I'll become a Sailing Smurf! Ha!
SPLASH
But I'M GOING TO SAIL!
?
?

END

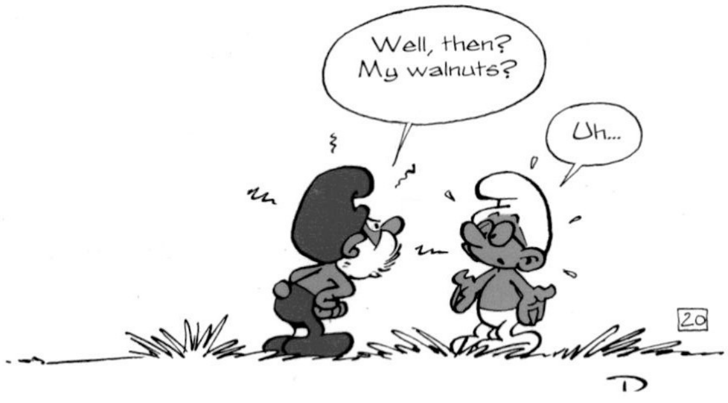
Well, then? My walnuts?
Uh...
20

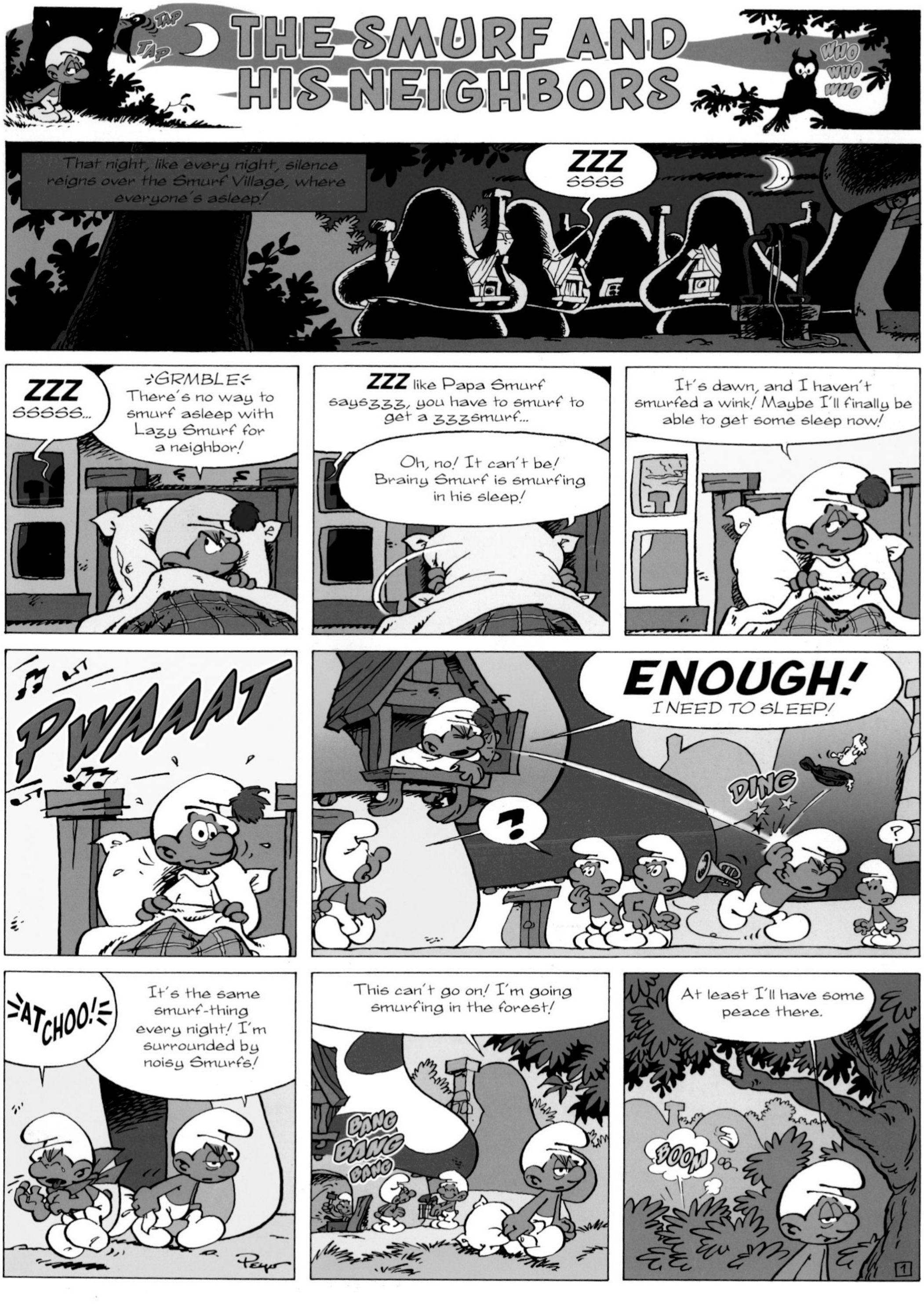
TAP
TAP
THE SMURF AND HIS NEIGHBORS
WHO WHO WHO
That night, like every night, silence reigns over the Smurf Village, where everyone's asleep!
ZZZ SSSS
ZZZ SSSSS...
GRMBLE
There's no way to smurf asleep with Lazy Smurf for a neighbor!
ZZZ like Papa Smurf says zzz, you have to smurf to get a zzzsmurf...
Oh, no! It can't be! Brainy Smurf is smurfing in his sleep!
It's dawn, and I haven't smurfed a wink! Maybe I'll finally be able to get some sleep now!
PWAAAT
ENOUGH! I NEED TO SLEEP!
?
DING
?
ATCHOO!
It's the same smurf-thing every night! I'm surrounded by noisy Smurfs!
Peyo
This can't go on! I'm going smurfing in the forest!
BANG BANG BANG
At least I'll have some peace there.
BOOM
1

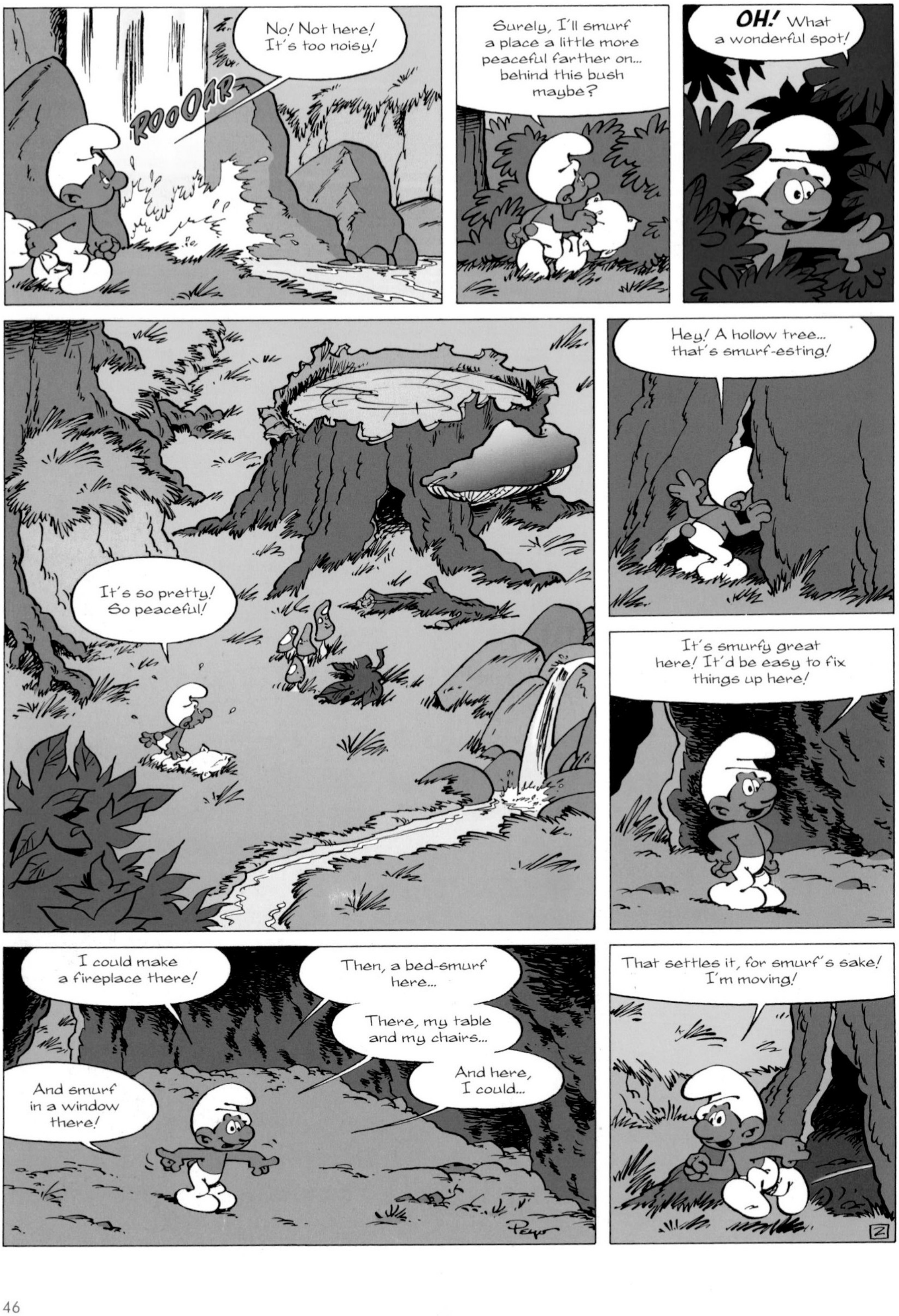

No! Not here! It's too noisy!
ROOOAR
Surely, I'll smurf a place a little more peaceful farther on... behind this bush maybe?
OH! What a wonderful spot!
It's so pretty! So peaceful!
Hey! A hollow tree... that's smurf-esting!
It's smurfy great here! It'd be easy to fix things up here!
I could make a fireplace there!
Then, a bed-smurf here...
There, my table and my chairs...
And here, I could...
And smurf in a window there!
Peyo
That settles it, for smurf's sake! I'm moving!
2

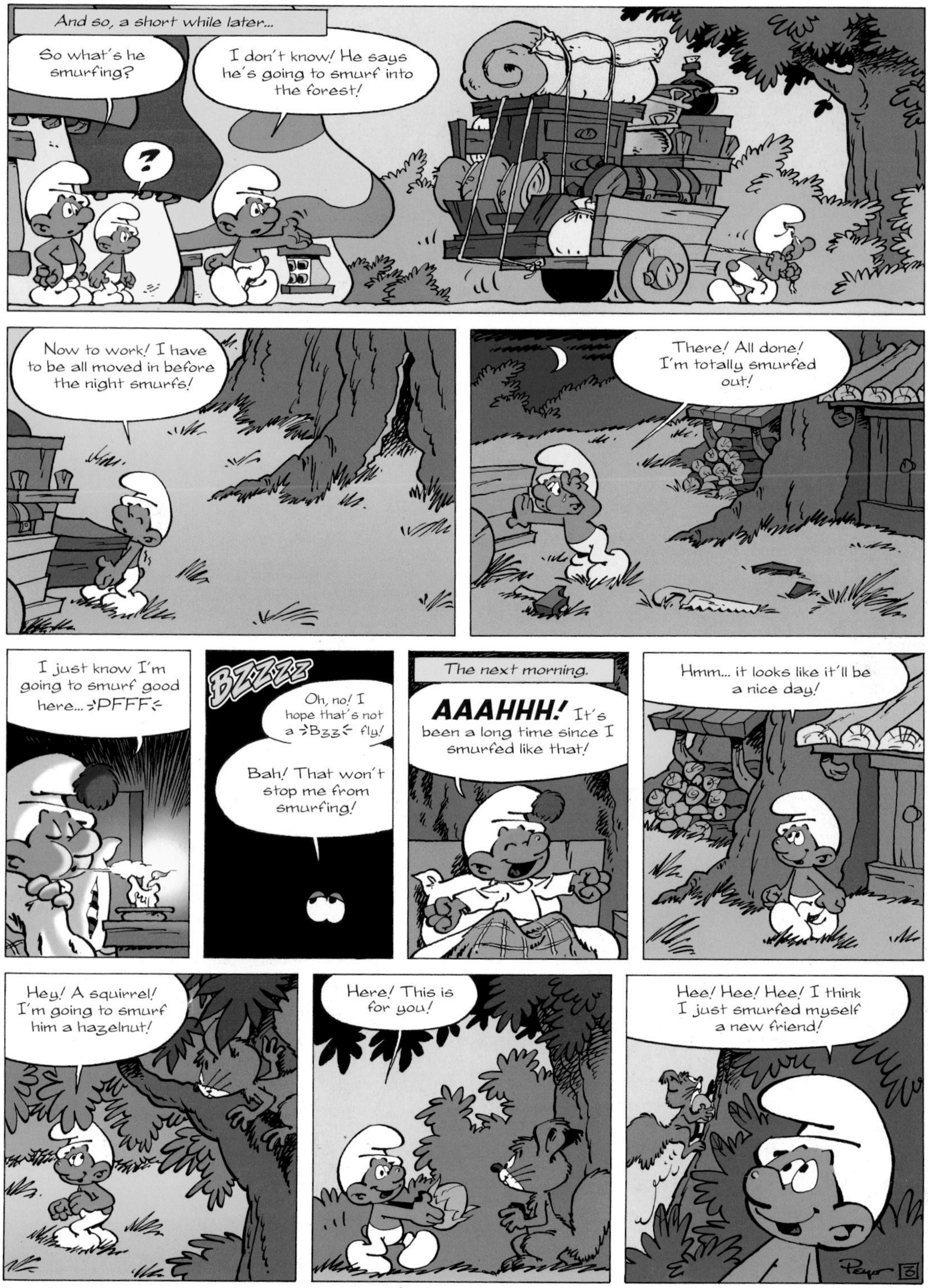
And so, a short while later...
So what's he smurfing?
I don't know! He says he's going to smurf into the forest!
?
Now to work! I have to be all moved in before the night smurfs!
There! All done! I'm totally smurfed out!
I just know I'm going to smurf good here... PFFF
BZZZZ
Oh, no! I hope that's not a Bzz fly!
Bah! That won't stop me from smurfing!
The next morning.
AAAHHH! It's been a long time since I smurfed like that!
Hmm... it looks like it'll be a nice day!
Hey! A squirrel! I'm going to smurf him a hazelnut!
Here! This is for you!
Hee! Hee! Hee! I think I just smurfed myself a new friend!
Peyo
3

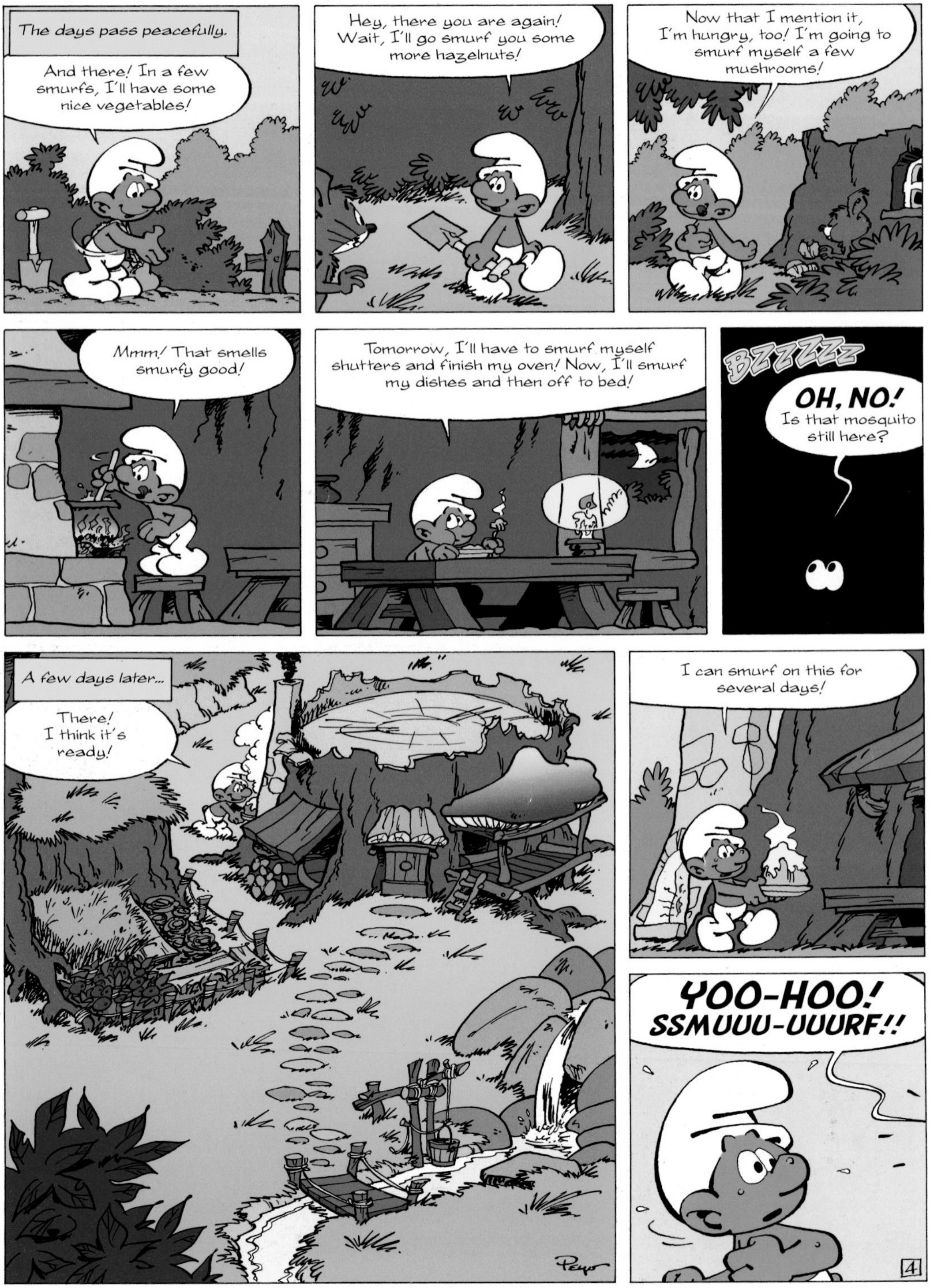
The days pass peacefully.
And there! In a few smurfs, I'll have some nice vegetables!
Hey, there you are again! Wait, I'll go smurf you some more hazelnuts!
Now that I mention it, I'm hungry, too! I'm going to smurf myself a few mushrooms!
Mmm! That smells smurfy good!
Tomorrow, I'll have to smurf myself shutters and finish my oven! Now, I'll smurf my dishes and then off to bed!
BZZZZZ
OH, NO! Is that mosquito still here?
A few days later...
There! I think it's ready!
Peyo
I can smurf on this for several days!
YOO-HOO! SSMUUU-UUURF!!
4

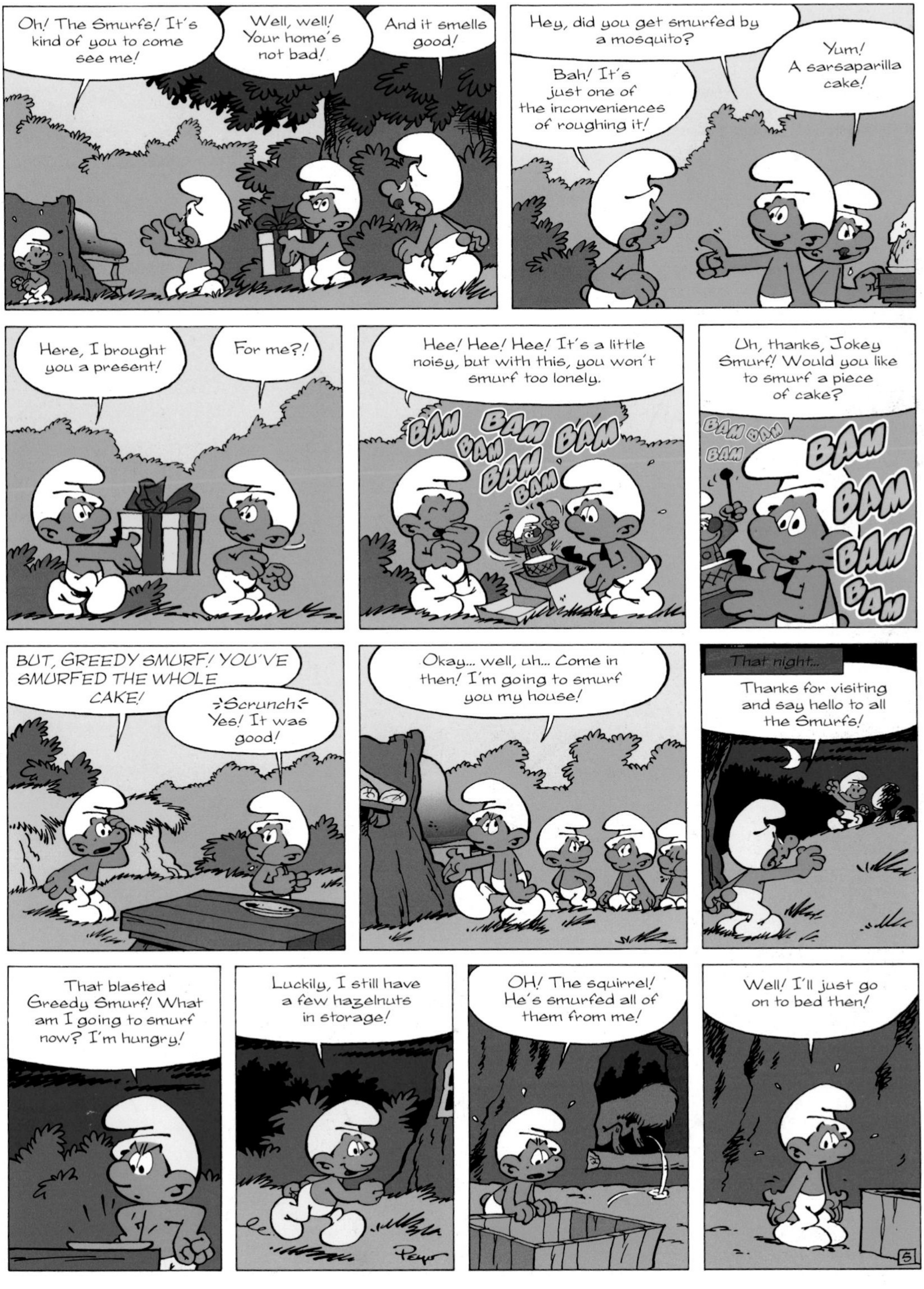

Oh! The Smurfs! It's kind of you to come see me!
Well, well! Your home's not bad!
And it smells good!
Hey, did you get smurfed by a mosquito?
Bah! It's just one of the inconveniences of roughing it!
Yum! A sarsaparilla cake!
Here, I brought you a present!
For me?!
Hee! Hee! Hee! It's a little noisy, but with this, you won't smurf too lonely.
BAM BAM BAM BAM BAM BAM BAM
Uh, thanks, Jokey Smurf! Would you like to smurf a piece of cake?
BAM BAM BAM BAM BAM BAM BAM BAM
BUT, GREEDY SMURF! YOU'VE SMURFED THE WHOLE CAKE!
Scrunch Yes! It was good!
Okay... well, uh... Come in then! I'm going to smurf you my house!
That night...
Thanks for visiting and say hello to all the Smurfs!
That blasted Greedy Smurf! What am I going to smurf now? I'm hungry!
Luckily, I still have a few hazelnuts in storage!
OH! The squirrel! He's smurfed all of them from me!
Well! I'll just go on to bed then!
5

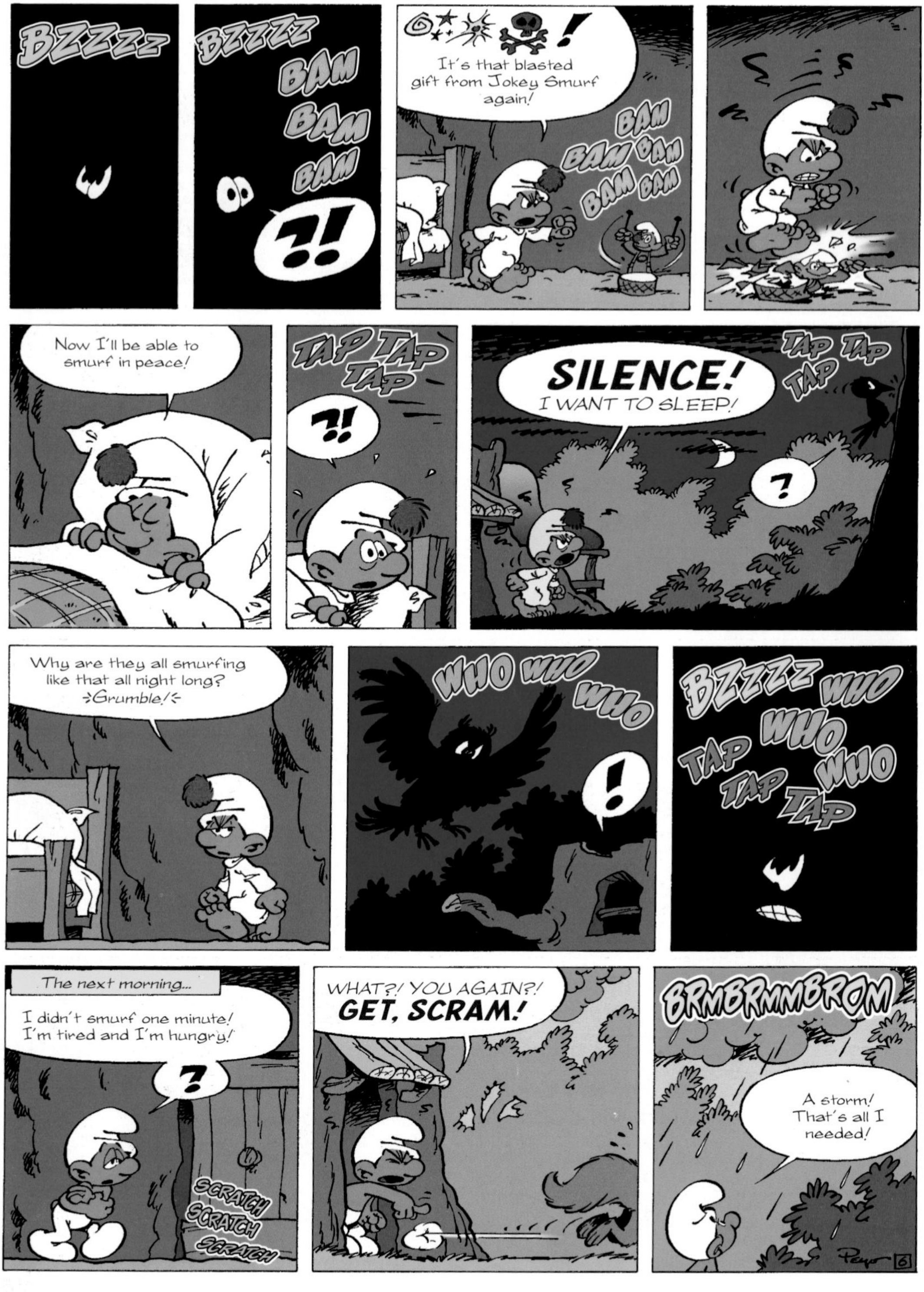
BZZZZZ
BZZZZZ
BAM
BAM
BAM
?!
It's that blasted gift from Jokey Smurf again!
BAM
BAM BAM
BAM BAM
Now I'll be able to smurf in peace!
TAP TAP TAP
?!
SILENCE!
I WANT TO SLEEP!
TAP TAP TAP
?
Why are they all smurfing like that all night long?
Grumble!
WHO WHO WHO
!
BZZZZ WHO
TAP WHO
TAP WHO
TAP
The next morning...
I didn't smurf one minute! I'm tired and I'm hungry!
?
SCRATCH
SCRATCH
SCRATCH
WHAT?! YOU AGAIN?!
GET, SCRAM!
BRMBRMMBROM
A storm! That's all I needed!
Peyo
6

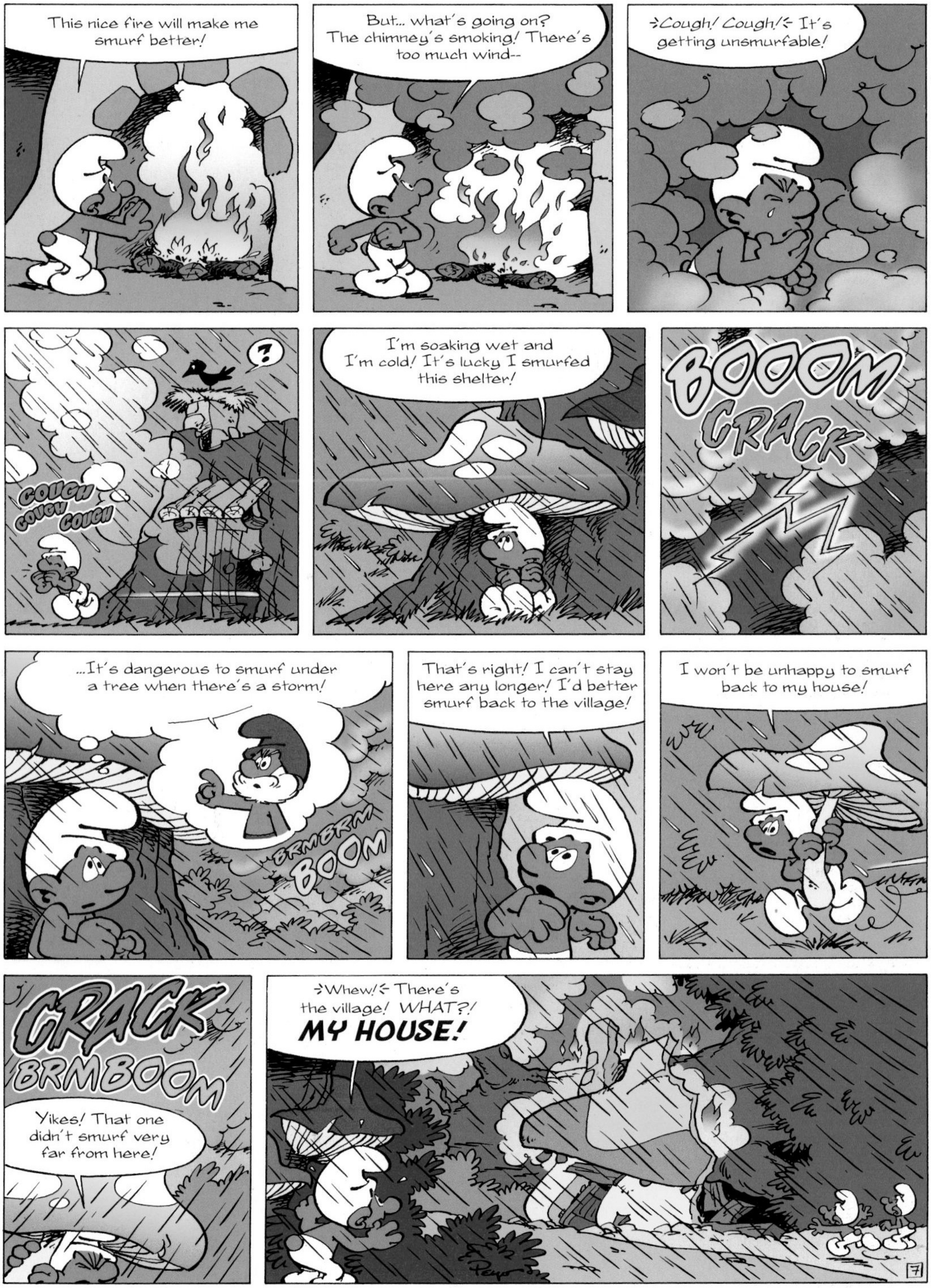
This nice fire will make me smurf better!
But... what's going on? The chimney's smoking! There's too much wind--
Cough! Cough! It's getting unsmurfable!
COUGH COUGH COUGH
?
I'm soaking wet and I'm cold! It's lucky I smurfed this shelter!
BOOOM CRACK
...It's dangerous to smurf under a tree when there's a storm!
BRMBRM BOOM
That's right! I can't stay here any longer! I'd better smurf back to the village!
I won't be unhappy to smurf back to my house!
CRACK BRMBOOM
Yikes! That one didn't smurf very far from here!
Whew! There's the village! WHAT?! **MY HOUSE!**
7

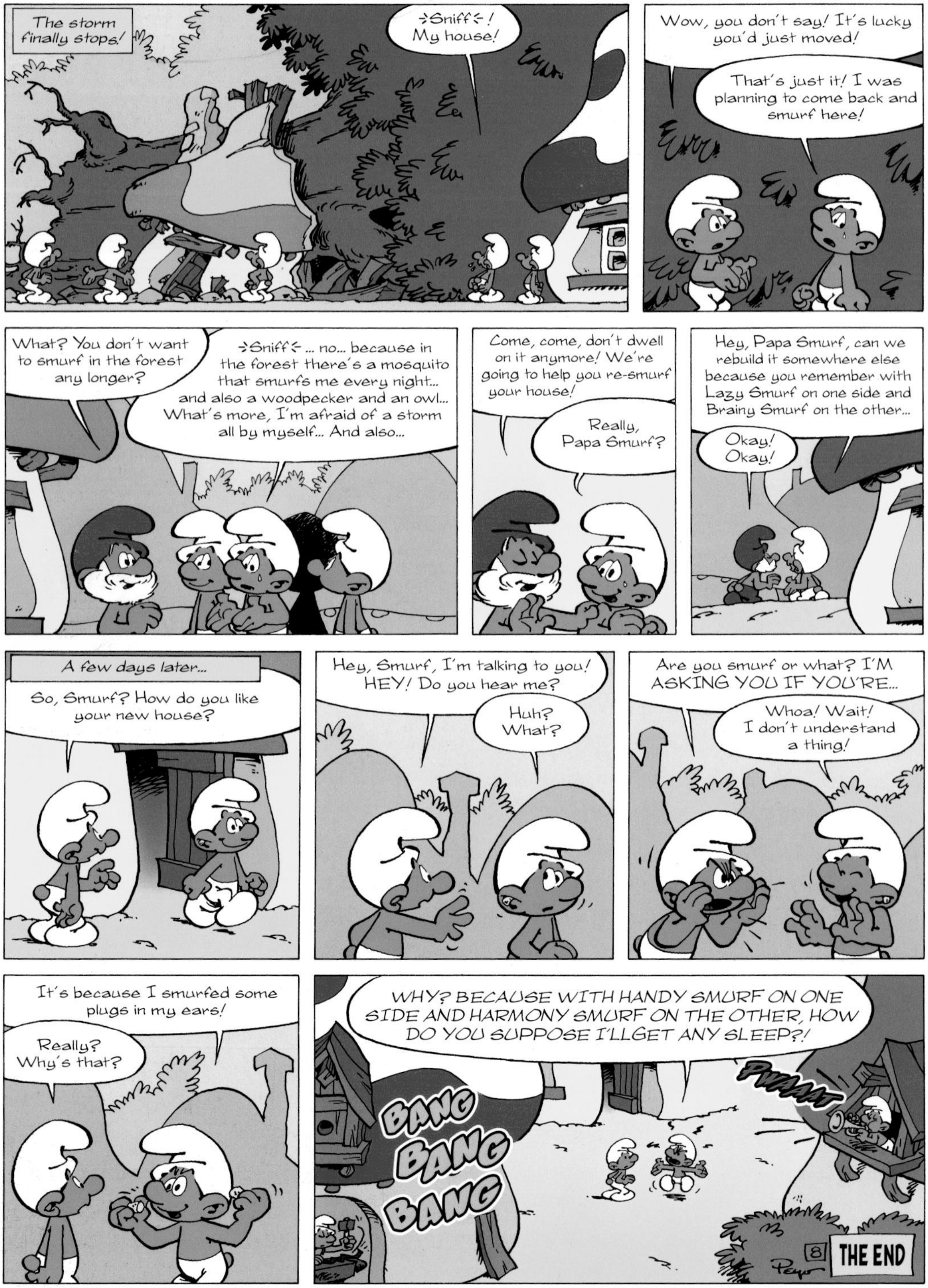

The storm finally stops!
Sniff! My house!
Wow, you don't say! It's lucky you'd just moved!
That's just it! I was planning to come back and smurf here!
What? You don't want to smurf in the forest any longer?
Sniff... no... because in the forest there's a mosquito that smurfs me every night... and also a woodpecker and an owl... What's more, I'm afraid of a storm all by myself... And also...
Come, come, don't dwell on it anymore! We're going to help you re-smurf your house!
Really, Papa Smurf?
Hey, Papa Smurf, can we rebuild it somewhere else because you remember with Lazy Smurf on one side and Brainy Smurf on the other...
Okay! Okay!
A few days later...
So, Smurf? How do you like your new house?
Hey, Smurf, I'm talking to you! HEY! Do you hear me?
Huh? What?
Are you smurf or what? I'M ASKING YOU IF YOU'RE...
Whoa! Wait! I don't understand a thing!
It's because I smurfed some plugs in my ears!
Really? Why's that?
WHY? BECAUSE WITH HANDY SMURF ON ONE SIDE AND HARMONY SMURF ON THE OTHER, HOW DO YOU SUPPOSE I'LLGET ANY SLEEP?!
BANG
BANG
BANG
PWAAAT
8
THE END

WATCH OUT FOR PAPERCUTZ™

Welcome to the first *Smurfs* graphic novel from Papercutz, the feisty little graphic novel publisher for all ages. I'm Jim Salicrup, the Smurf-in-Chief, and all of us here at Papercutz are thrilled to be bringing back the classic Smurfs comics by Peyo to a North American audience. Not everyone realizes that the Smurfs originally appeared in comics, and were later adapted into animated films and TV series, not to mention toys. In fact, the Smurfs made their debut in a graphic album called "Johan et Pirlouit" in 1958. We decided to publish that historic debut of the Smurfs, in our second Smurfs graphic novel—"The Smurfs and the Magic Flute"—but be warned, that the stars of the story are Johan and Peewit. The Smurfs don't appear in the first half of the story. Of course, when they do appear, they're truly magical.

As for this smurfilicious volume, there's an interesting story there too. The original title for the first story is "Les Schtroumpfs Noirs" or "The Black Smurfs," and it's never been published in English before. The reason is that there was a concern that the story would be misinterpreted and be found offensive to African-Americans. While we believe that there is nothing at all racist about the story, we can see how the story could very easily be taken the wrong way, especially by children. We decided to follow the lead of the Hanna-Barbera animation studio back when they adapted the story, and simply changed the black smurfs to purple smurfs. Since this was already done before, in animated form, we like to therefore believe that Peyo would've approved.

If you're wondering about that orange cat who appears on page two of "The Flying Smurf," that's Azrael, the pet of the wicked sorcerer Gargamel. The first story to feature the Smurf's arch foe, "The Smurfnapper," is featured in THE SMURFS #9 "Gargamel and the Smurfs," as well as in THE SMURFS ANTHOLOGY Volume 1.

Right now seems to be a great time for Smurf fans. Papercutz is bringing back the original comics, the Hanna-Barbera cartoons continue to run on Cartoon Network's Boomerang network and are available on DVDs, and all-new, star-studded, major Hollywood movies starring Neil Patrick Harris, Sofia Vergara, Hank Azaria (as Gargamel), and featuring the voices of Katy Perry (as Smurfette), Alan Cumming, Paul Reubens (not as Peewit, but as Jokey Smurf), George Lopez, Jeff Foxworthy, John Oliver, and Jonathan Winters (as Papa Smurf) are introducting new generations to our little blue buddies. What more could you possibly ask for?

So until next time, be sure to visit papercutz.com for further Smurfs comics news, and stay Smurfy!

Thanks,
Jim

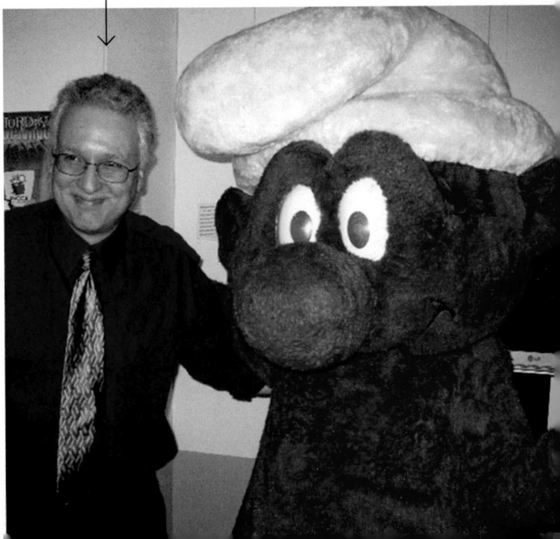

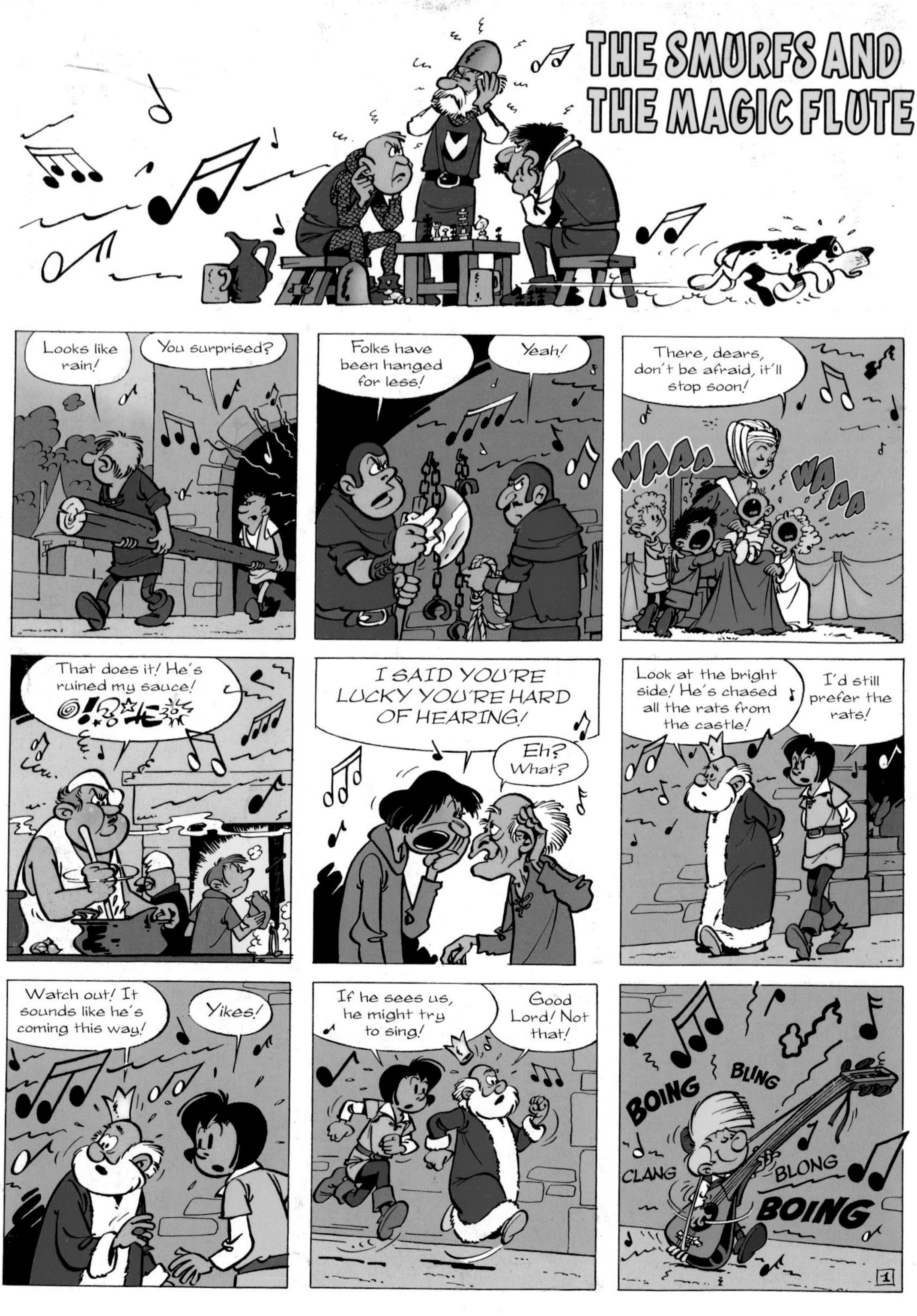
THE SMURFS AND THE MAGIC FLUTE
Looks like rain!
You surprised?
Folks have been hanged for less!
Yeah!
There, dears, don't be afraid, it'll stop soon!
WAAA
WAAA
That does it! He's ruined my sauce!
I SAID YOU'RE LUCKY YOU'RE HARD OF HEARING!
Eh? What?
Look at the bright side! He's chased all the rats from the castle!
I'd still prefer the rats!
Watch out! It sounds like he's coming this way!
Yikes!
If he sees us, he might try to sing!
Good Lord! Not that!
BOING
BLING
CLANG
BLONG
BOING
1

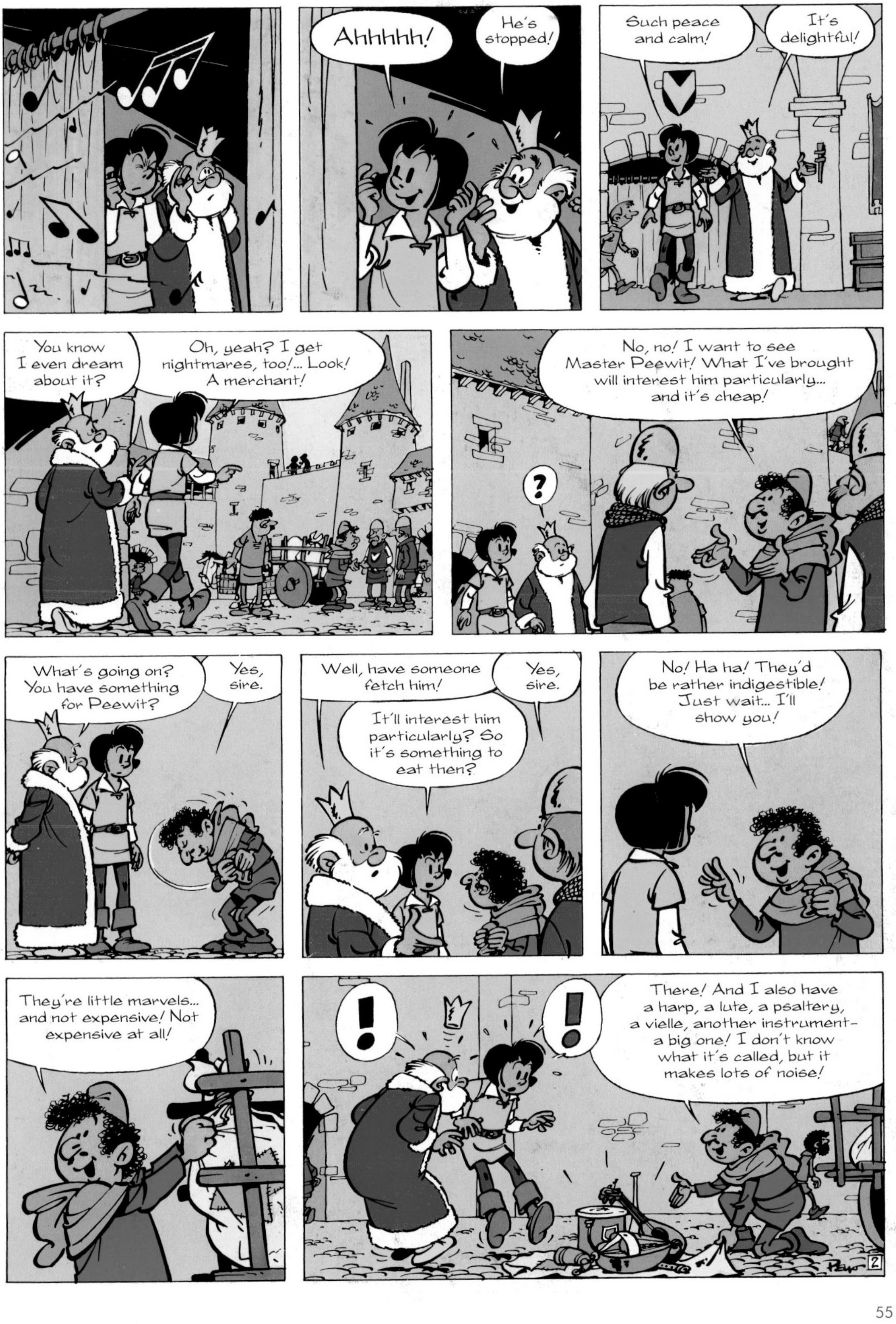
Ahhhhh!
He's stopped!
Such peace and calm!
It's delightful!
You know I even dream about it?
Oh, yeah? I get nightmares, too!... Look! A merchant!
No, no! I want to see Master Peewit! What I've brought will interest him particularly... and it's cheap!
?
What's going on? You have something for Peewit?
Yes, sire.
Well, have someone fetch him!
Yes, sire.
It'll interest him particularly? So it's something to eat then?
No! Ha ha! They'd be rather indigestible! Just wait... I'll show you!
They're little marvels... and not expensive! Not expensive at all!
!
!
There! And I also have a harp, a lute, a psaltery, a vielle, another instrument- a big one! I don't know what it's called, but it makes lots of noise!

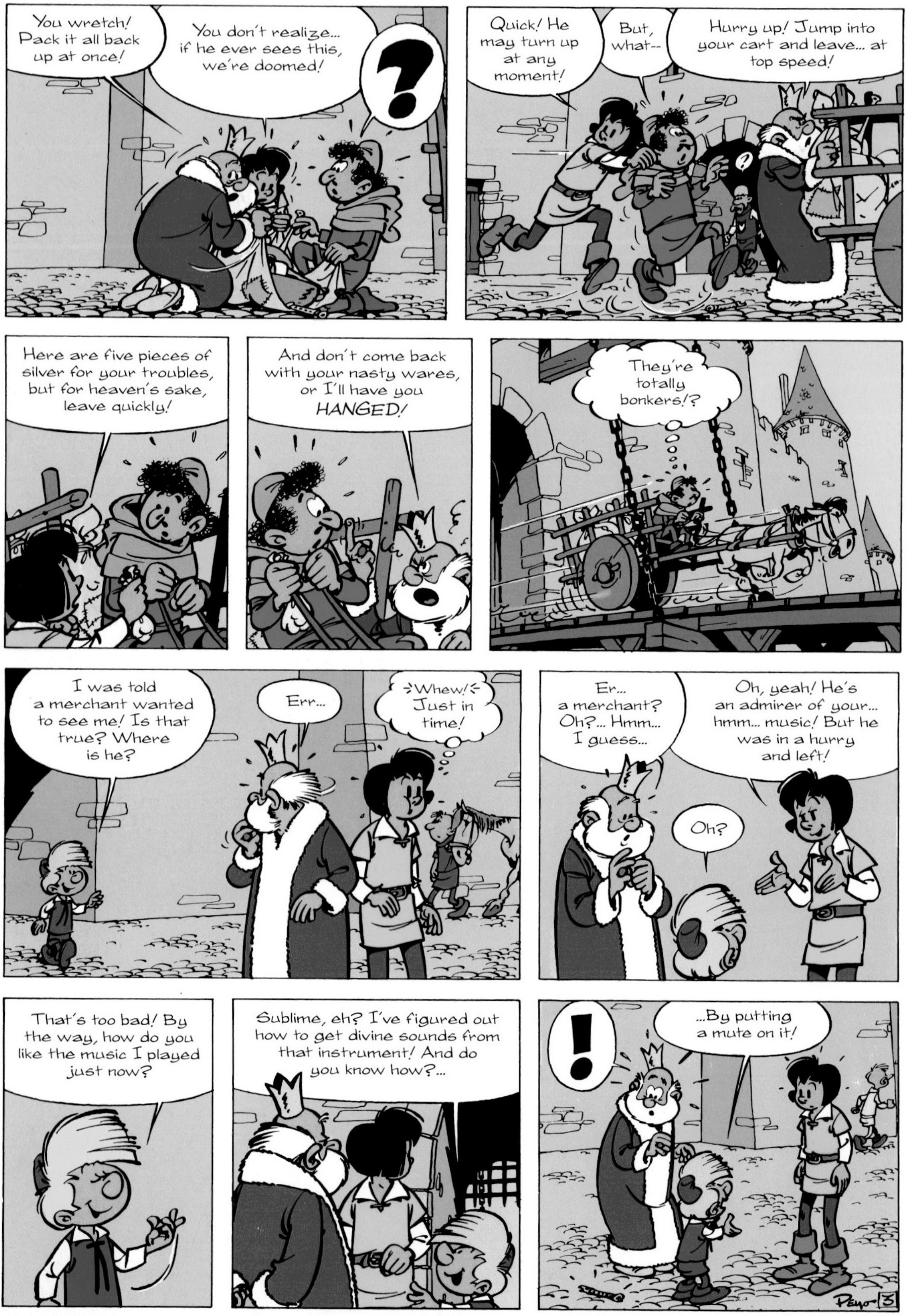

You wretch! Pack it all back up at once!
You don't realize... if he ever sees this, we're doomed!
?
Quick! He may turn up at any moment!
But, what--
Hurry up! Jump into your cart and leave... at top speed!
Here are five pieces of silver for your troubles, but for heaven's sake, leave quickly!
And don't come back with your nasty wares, or I'll have you HANGED!
They're totally bonkers!?
I was told a merchant wanted to see me! Is that true? Where is he?
Err...
Whew! Just in time!
Er... a merchant? Oh?... Hmm... I guess...
Oh, yeah! He's an admirer of your... hmm... music! But he was in a hurry and left!
Oh?
That's too bad! By the way, how do you like the music I played just now?
Sublime, eh? I've figured out how to get divine sounds from that instrument! And do you know how?...
!
...By putting a mute on it!
Peyo
3

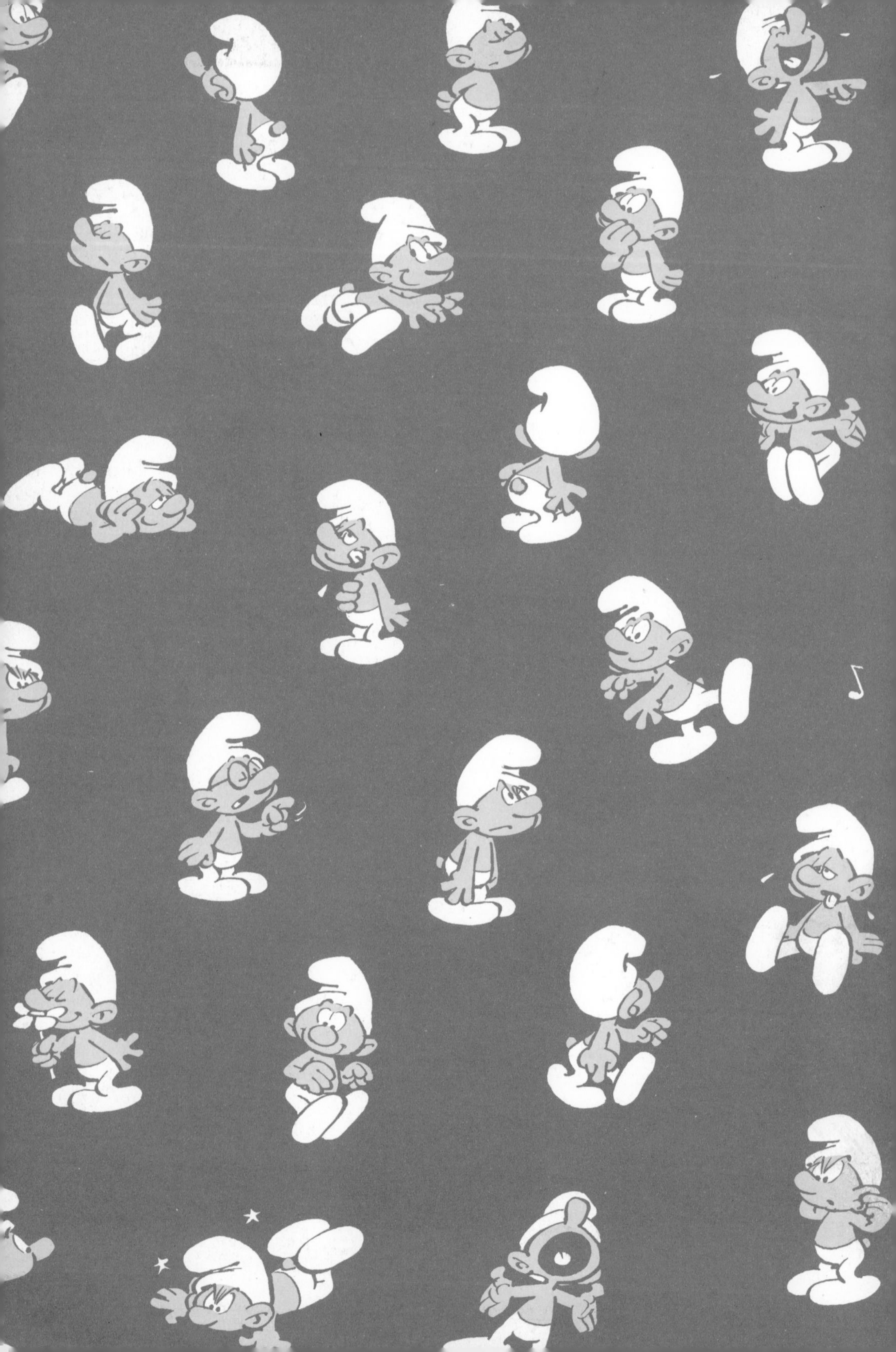